ALEX IN THE ANNEX

JEREMY D SCHOLZ

For information, permissions, or bulk-order inquiries, contact: Moxie Books, Mesa, Arizona

Moxie-Books.com

Paperback ISBN: 979-8-9994313-3-2

Hardback ISBN: 979-8-9994313-6-3

Printed in the United States of America

First Edition

Magnus and the Last Dragon by Jeremy D. Scholz

Published by Moxie Books - Mesa, Arizona

http://Moxie-Books.com

From the very beginning, you've been my first listener, my most honest critic, and my biggest fan.

You laughed in the right places, asked the best questions, and always wanted to hear what happened next. That kind of curiosity is the greatest gift a storyteller could ever hope for.

When I doubted myself, you reminded me to keep going.

When I wanted to give up, you reminded me why I started.

And when the stories grew quiet, your encouragement brought them back to life.

This book, like so many of my words, is woven through with your love and belief in me.

I dedicate these pages to you, Molly, because without you, they might never have existed.

Thank you for reminding me that stories matter, and that the best ones are shared with the people we love most.

INTRODUCTION

Every school has a place students aren't supposed to go. And Theodore Roosevelt Jr. High was no different. It's place was the a chained-off hallway whispered about in rumors, forgotten by teachers, and avoided by everyone else.

As a kid, I practically wished for something exciting to happen during the mind-numbing days of school. Bring on the zombie apocalypse, the invasion by a foreign country, the alien abduction, or even a superpower.

As an adult, I still dream about flying away from the same boredom, only now, it's in the workplace. I hope you connect to the desire to be more than what you are. Escapism is what reading and now writing stories is all about.

Let's join in one morning, when boredom turns into adventure. Where Alex and his best friend Rachelle find a forgotten wing of their junior high, locked away and abandoned. Everything screams, stay out.

Lets Begin

J.S.

EARLY RISERS CLUB

"Great, just great, I get to be a loner walking the halls," Alex thought as he waved goodbye to his mom.

He walked up the steps to the entrance of his school. There it was looming in front of him. Theodore Roosevelt Jr. High. It was mostly unremarkable, probably like every other school in the country. It was mostly just the background to his existence. He had to come to school early today. His mother had an early meeting and dropped him off on her way. He could have walked and got there at a regular time, but what self-respecting 8th grader was going to walk when a ride was possible? Now at the gates, he wondered if he had made a mistake.

He looked back and was surprised to see Rachelle

walking up the sidewalk towards him. He was relieved to not be alone. Rachelle had been a friend since kindergarten. She was fun; she had no problem being silly. He liked it because he tended to be too random for most people's taste. Not Rachelle; she seemed to enjoy matching his energy. Alex remembered all the dumb games and roleplaying they had done back in elementary school. Alex snapped out of it as she walked up.

"Hey Alex, how come you're so early?" she asked.

"Mom had a meeting and had to go to work early," he said with a shrug.

"Why are you early?"

"My brother drops me off. He has basketball practice, so I'll be early all this quarter." Her face looked annoyed.

"Oh, that's lame. I was worried I was going to be alone this morning. I can't imagine being alone every morning." He meant to show he understood the gravity of the situation.

She just rolled her eyes, the universal sign of teenage girls for: not happy with what was just said.

Alex pushed the gate open and held it for her.

"What should we do?" Alex asked.

"I was going to go to the library and read, but that's because I planned on being by myself," she said. "Do you have another idea?"

"I don't know. Let's walk around and see what we find." Alex headed down the hall.

Rachelle fell in step beside him, her backpack bouncing slightly with each stride. "So... campus tour? Led by two unqualified guides who just got here?"

"Yep," Alex said with a grin. "Guided misadventure."

The school was oddly quiet, with just a few muffled voices and the hum of fluorescent lights buzzing above. The main hallway stretched ahead like a tunnel, with lockers on both sides in various states of sticker-decoration and some with minor dents. The air smelled of freshly polished floors and something vaguely cafeteria-ish.

Their first stop was the trophy case. It towered to the ceiling, its ancient wood badly in need of conditioning. They both stopped in front of it like they'd stumbled upon a sacred shrine.

"Is that a bowling trophy?" Rachelle asked, squinting.

Alex leaned closer. "Yep. Roosevelt Jr. High: District Champions, 1993."

Rachelle let out a small, delighted gasp. "That's such a specific flex. I love it."

Alex grinned. "Should we pay our respects to the bowling gods?"

They both gave mock bows to the dusty trophy and laughed at their cleverness. Alex did feel an unspoken regret, realizing he had yet to make his mark. The trophies made him evaluate what he had accomplished at the school. He shook it off as they continued on their impromptu tour.

They passed the auditorium, doors slightly ajar, so of course they peeked in to see rows of empty seats and a giant painted canvas for a play called Hercules: The Musical. In the center of the canvas was a poorly drawn centaur who looked like he regretted every life choice.

Alex pointed. "Now that's art."

They both snorted and wandered on, down the hall.

In the science wing, they found a poster board left behind from some class project titled How Volcanoes Can Kill You. The font was all bubbly and cheerful, and the little cartoon volcano had angry eyes and lava like spaghetti. Rachelle took a picture of it with her phone.

"New lock screen. Wait, you hold it up," she said.

He held it up, trying miserably to match the angry eyes. She framed the picture so that he was the focus. She smiled to herself when she looked at the picture of Alex. She snapped herself out of it before Alex could notice.

They passed the band room, which was locked, but they could hear the faint drone of a tuba. Somewhere, someone was practicing poorly and unapologetically. Rachelle blew out her cheeks, trying to match her face to the sound.

"I bet that kid is confident," Alex said. "You have to be, to fail that loudly."

"I respect it better than the ones that never try," Rachelle replied.

It was an off-the-cuff comment, but it stung Alex more than he expected. He quietly wished he had taken more chances. He recognized he tended to always take the safe path.

They turned a corner and discovered something unexpected.

A hallway they had never noticed before. It was narrower, dimmer, and seemed to stretch toward the end of the wing where only Mr. Willy's classroom was supposed to be.

"Has this always been here?" Alex asked.

Rachelle just shrugged.

The lights here flickered as if they hadn't been replaced since the 90s. At the end of the hall stood a set of old double doors, their metal-frames were grimy at the edges, and there was a massive, rusted chain wrapped around the crash bars.

They stopped a few feet away and looked around, trying to get their bearings straight.

Rachelle looked for something familiar. "Where are we?"

"Well, that's... ominous," Alex said, looking at the double doors.

Rachelle crossed her arms. "Very horror movie vibes. What do you think is back there? Boiler room? Secret principal dungeon?"

"Detention for kids who skip too many assemblies," Alex offered.

They looked at each other. Then, naturally, Alex tried the door. It didn't budge at first, but after some wiggling, he managed to open it just enough for them to peek through. The chain groaned but held.

"Shhh, don't Alex, I mean—It's chained for a reason." Rachelle took a step back. Something about the door made her uneasy, like foreshadowing some unseen looming disaster.

Behind the door was another wing, completely dark. No emergency lights, no glow from windows. Just rows of doors and a faint echo, like the building was remembering its own ghosts.

"Whoa," Rachelle whispered.

Alex pressed his face to the crack. "What is this place?"

There were desks still in there, covered in dust. A forgotten water fountain. A torn poster about internet safety.

"Maybe it's the old wing," Rachelle said. "My brother told me something about part of the school being shut down after a pipe burst when he was here."

Alex backed away. "We have to come back here.

Who knows what we could find in there? I mean, we could be famous if we uncover something amazing. We will need flashlights."

"And snacks," Rachelle added. "In case we get trapped."

He gave her a puzzled look. "That's your first thought? Snacks?"

"Look, I don't mind being the kid who dies of boredom in a haunted junior high building, but I'm not going to starve. Snacks are important."

They laughed and walked back toward the main hall. They emerged from the darkened end of the hallway. No one else seemed to notice, but they saw Mr. Willy unlocking his classroom.

A few other early students were starting to trickle in. The building was waking up. The normal chaos that was jr high was about to start.

"Thanks for walking around with me," Rachelle said, bumping his shoulder with hers.

"Thanks for not reading in the library alone like a tragic nerd," he chided her back.

She laughed. "Shut up."

He smiled. He didn't say it out loud, but this morning was already better than he'd expected.

The buzz of voices grew louder as more kids filed through the front doors. Backpacks rustled, sneakers squeaked, and lockers clanged open and shut. The sleepy stillness of the morning was officially over.

"Yo!" a voice called from down the hall.

Alex turned just in time to see Lucas and Hudson walking toward them. Lucas had his usual hoodie pulled over a graphic tee that probably meant something obscure. His black hair was cut in a jagged fringe that hung just above sharp, observant eyes, deep brown, nearly black. Lucas didn't miss much. Hudson was hard to miss; his height and size tended to make him stand out. He had earbuds in, and his head bobbed slightly to music only he could hear.

"What's up with the early risers club? When did you guys even get here?" Lucas asked, stretching his arms over his head with a yawn.

"Come on, more like an involuntary early risers club. We've been here since six," Rachelle said, grinning.

Alex gave them a quick recap. "We've been exploring. We found a volcano poster that wants to kill you, a haunted trophy case, and the old wing of the school chained up like something out of Scooby-Doo."

Lucas's eyes lit up. "You found the annex?"

"The what?" Rachelle blinked.

Lucas leaned against the wall, clearly pleased to be the one with answers. "The annex. It used to be part of the school — classrooms, science labs, even a weird little greenhouse on the roof. But they shut it down forever ago. My oldest brother was in 8th grade when they closed it off."

Alex perked up. "How do you always know things? Do you know why they shut it?"

"Of course I do," Lucas expounded, "Something about a pipe bursting. Flooded half the building. Mold, bad wiring, all that stuff. The district said it was too expensive to fix."

Hudson popped out one earbud. "Yeah, my cousin said it smells like old mop water and lost dreams."

Rachelle made a face. "That's oddly poetic."

Alex looked back down the hallway, almost as though he could see through the walls to the chained-up double doors. "We peeked through. It's still full of desks and posters. Totally dark."

"Of course it is," Lucas said. "It's a relic. Time capsule. No one goes in there."

Hudson smirked. "Well, no one officially."

That made all four of them pause for a second. The unspoken idea was already settling between them like a plan forming on its own. Their curiosity raced into overdrive.

"It would be cool to see what's in there. What if we made a meaningful discovery?" Alex mused.

"Yeah, well," Lucas added, his voice dropping to mock seriousness, "if someone were to investigate, they'd want to do it when there aren't teachers everywhere."

"Like after school?" Rachelle asked.

Alex gave a slow nod. "Or early. Like... today."

"I don't know if I want to join the early risers club; I do love my sleep," Lucas said.

"You do need more beauty sleep." Hudson jabbed at Lucas.

They all turned and glanced back toward the front entrance where the flow of students continued, and the bell was only minutes from ringing. The world was waking up, rules were tightening, and the annex would soon be forgotten again.

The bell rang, shrill and immediate, pulling them back into the rhythm of a regular school day.

"Here we go." Rachelle rolled her eyes.

FIRST PERIOD WAS SOCIAL STUDIES, which meant beige walls, a clock that ticked too loudly, and Mr. Willy's monotone voice filling the air like fog. The desks were in neat rows, and the four friends were scattered throughout the room. Teachers never let the "talkers" sit together. It was a rule Alex had learned the hard way.

Alex sat near the back, two rows behind Rachelle, with Hudson diagonally across the room and Lucas near the windows, already doodling in the margins of his notebook like it was a part-time job.

Mr. Willy droned on about trade routes and something to do with the Silk Road. Alex's eyes drifted toward the ceiling tiles, then back down to Rachelle. She was sitting straight, pretending to listen, but he caught the subtle flick of her fingers against her thigh: three taps, then a quick swipe across her knee.

Alex's lips twitched into a grin. That meant **"bored out of my skull."**

He tapped the side of his pencil once, paused, then tapped again. **"Same."**

From the window side, Lucas coughed, just once, but he followed it with a stretch that ended with two fingers raised like rabbit ears behind his head. Classic **"plan later?"**

Alex casually scratched his neck in response, flashing one finger, then two. **"Period two, hall lockers."**

Across the room, Hudson tapped his pencil once, delayed, tapped again. **"Agreed."**

The teacher didn't seem to notice. Mr. Willy was too busy asking a question no one wanted to answer.

"Can anyone explain the economic importance of the Silk Road?"

Silence.

Alex risked a glance at Hudson, who was now

slumped dramatically in his seat with his eyes half-closed. Lucas had his chin resting on his fist, pretending to be deep in thought. Rachelle, to her credit, raised her hand halfway before lowering it again like she remembered she didn't actually care.

Mr. Willey sighed. "No? Anyone?"

Alex slowly raised his hand and felt three sets of invisible stares land on him.

"Yes, Alex?"

He cleared his throat. "It connected places. So, people could trade. Things like... silk. And spices. And probably boredom."

A few kids laughed. Mr. Willy gave him a sharp look. "Thank you for that...."

Alex leaned back, for a moment unnerved by the look in Mr. Willy's eyes.

He tapped his desk lightly, one knock, then a circle traced on the wood.

"We've got this."

Rachelle made the tiniest heart with her fingers. Lucas mock-gagged and hid it with a cough. Hudson twirled his pencil like a ninja staff.

It was their version of a group text. Silent, ridiculous, and understandable only to them. They had started using signals in grade school, and it had developed into a language all its own. Developed in the minds of four children, it was quite chaotic, but they were all fluent. Words and phrases were added as needed at the whim of the one needing to say it.

As Mr. Willey returned to his slides, Alex settled into his seat. The annex mystery was still sitting in the back of his mind like a puzzle waiting to be picked apart, but for now, he had a mission: get through class without falling asleep... and meet at the lockers after second period.

As Mr. Willy droned on, Alex's eyes drifted again, not to the ceiling this time, but across the room to the left in the front row, where Charlotte was sitting.

Charlotte Novikova.

Even her name felt like she was descended from a royal line.

She had transferred sometime last year, and by now she was fully cemented in the social hierarchy as one of those girls — pretty, confident, always surrounded by people. She already looked like a high schooler, and Alex was convinced she lived in a world entirely different from his. From the day she started at Theodore Roosevelt Jr. High, she was sucked in by the "It" crowd.

She was sitting at her desk now, half-listening, twirling a lock of shiny blonde hair around her finger like it was an unconscious art form. The sunlight through the windows hit her just right, and for a second, Alex forgot what century the Silk Road was even in. She was perfect. Like... a work of art, perfect. Her posture. Her handwriting. Even the way she clicked her pen was kind of elegant.

Alex didn't stand a chance. Not in any real way. Not unless he suddenly grew five inches, gained a sense of charisma, and stopped tripping over his own sentences.

But he could look.

And so he did.

Just long enough to feel that weird mix of awe and guilt that always came with crushes. He knew he'd never get to talk to her. What would he even say? "Hi, I noticed you're a fully realized human person and I'm a quaking pile of anxiety. Want to hang out sometime?"

Yeah. No.

He was somewhere deep in a completely unrealistic fantasy, maybe one where she needed help with her locker and he was inexplicably cool and clever, when her head turned. Their eyes met. For one terrifying second, Charlotte blinked. Then she tilted her head slightly. Not in a mean way, but in that wait, were you just looking at me? kind of way. Her eyebrows lifted in a quizzical arch.

Alex's brain tripped over itself.

Abort! Abort!

He snapped his eyes forward, stared down at his textbook like it had just burst into flames, and tried to casually rub his forehead like he'd just been... thinking really hard?

Great. Now she thinks I'm weird. Or creepy. Or both. Probably both.

He didn't dare look again. His ears were burning.

From the corner of his vision, he saw Lucas glance over and smirk like he'd caught the whole thing. Alex flicked his eyes up just long enough to give him the universal "shut up" look.

Mr. Willy clapped his hands once. "Alex the Annex is calling."

Alex shook his head. Had he just heard that? No one else seemed to have heard it. He looked at his teacher with eyes struggling to recall something they had missed.

Mr. Willy just smiled at him. "Alright, folks, let's do some group notes. Pair up with someone around you."

Alex let out a quiet sigh of relief. Group work. A temporary distraction from the flaming wreckage of his social confidence.

And maybe, maybe, a chance to stop thinking about Charlotte Novikova before he melted into the floor.

The end of first period bell rang, and the usual herd of students poured into the hallway like a broken dam. Backpacks thudded against lockers, sneakers squeaked on the tile, and the volume jumped five levels in a matter of seconds.

Alex headed toward his locker, threading through the crowd. Rachelle was already there, leaning against the metal door beside his, picking at the corner of a sticker someone had half-peeled off. She looked up as he approached.

"You looked like you were about to fall into a coma," she said.

"I was deep in historical reflection," Alex said with a straight face. Then, under his breath, "Also, Charlotte looked at me. So... I died briefly."

Rachelle raised an eyebrow but didn't comment on that. She just gave a noncommittal "hmm."

Lucas and Hudson strolled up a few seconds later. Lucas was eating something straight from his hoodie pocket, possibly fruit snacks, possibly something he found there this morning. Lucas shoved Alex with a knowing nod, but to his credit he didn't say anything.

"So," Lucas said between chews, "this annex thing. I don't think I can make it work."

Alex blinked. "Why?"

"Yeah," Hudson chimed in. "We've got robotics club this week, and I kinda need to start showing up to it. Also, if I get caught sneaking into a sealed-off building, my mom's gonna kill me. Like, in a very legal, premeditated way."

Alex looked between them, a little surprised. "But

we were going to check it out. The place is practically begging to be explored."

"Yeah, I mean… maybe," Lucas said, stuffing the rest of his snack into his mouth. "But it's probably just mold and old desks. The idea of it was cool, but I doubt we would find anything."

"Plus," Hudson added, "we can probably Google what it looked like. There's like, historical yearbook stuff online."

Alex glanced at Rachelle, expecting her to nod and bail too.

Instead, she just shrugged. "I kind of want to see."

Alex blinked. "Really?"

She shifted her backpack on her shoulder. "I mean… It sounds fun. You know. Weird, mysterious, possibly dangerous. Kind of your thing."

He caught the small smile tugging at the edge of her mouth. "So you're only in because I want to?"

"I didn't say that," she said, picking at the locker sticker again. "But yes. Obviously."

Alex grinned. "Okay then. We'll go. Just us."

Lucas mock-saluted. "Good luck dying of asbestos poisoning. Let us know if you see a ghost janitor or something."

Hudson added, "Text me if you need bail money. My mom has a lawyer."

Rachelle looked at Alex as the other two wandered off. "So when do we sneak in?"

"Before school?" Alex said. "We are here before anyone anyways. Bring a flashlight."

"And snacks," Rachelle added. "Because I refuse to break and enter on an empty stomach."

He laughed. "Deal."

She bumped his shoulder with hers as they started down the hall together. "Also... you might want to work on your subtle staring."

His face turned red instantly. "I wasn't..."

"Uh-huh."

Alex just pushed her into the lockers. She smiled, not mean, just amused. And he smiled too, but inside, something fluttered a little in his chest. Maybe the annex wasn't the only mystery he'd be exploring at school.

He did love that Rachelle was always down for what he wanted to do. She had been his closest friend since kindergarten.

2

CLASSIFIED CURIOSITY

When Alex arrived at school, it was early — the kind of early that made everything feel quieter than it should be. He was excited and wasn't even sure why, other than it was a risk. He wanted to take a risk; he was tired of playing it safe. He checked the time several times. *Where are you?* Rachelle should have been here by now.

Rachelle: My brother's sick. No early

drop-off. I'll be there later. Sorry, I
wanted to be there. :(

Damn! Alex hesitated for a few seconds. Rachelle would have been there if it was up to her. Being at the mercy of parents and older siblings was one of the lamest parts of jr high. He grabbed his backpack, made sure the flashlight worked, and slipped through the gate. He bounded up the steps and through the front door.

His footsteps echoed down the empty hallway as he moved quickly toward the forgotten corridor. Past the trophy case, the auditorium, and the science room. He looked to see no one was watching and ducked into the dim hallway.

Now, standing in front of the chained double doors, he pulled the small padlock into view. The chain was rusty, but the lock itself was newer, probably replaced sometime in the last few years, as though someone still wanted to keep people out.

Well, not today. Alex was done waiting for others to make things happen.

Alex reached into his jacket pocket and pulled out two metal hairpins. His mom would never notice they were missing. He'd been up most of the night watching video tutorials on how to pick padlocks, mostly from guys named "LockPickingLawyer" and "Urban Survival Guru." They made it look easy.

It was not easy.

His fingers were numb from the morning chill, and he was nervous. He felt the tiny internal click, and the lock popped open.

He stared at it for a second, then let out a quiet, victorious "Yes!"

He had halfway doubted he would even be able to get in, but now, nothing was standing in the way. For a brief moment, he considered waiting for someone else to be able to come too. Playing it safe again, he heard in his mind.

"No!" he said to himself.

He unwrapped the chain and slipped through the door, shoving the lock deep into his pocket. No way was he getting trapped in here. Not until he knew what 'here' was all about. *Wish Rachelle were here. I wish someone were here.* If something went wrong, he was on his own.

From the moment he stepped in, the annex was everything he had hoped for, and more. The rush of being somewhere forbidden had a thrilling aspect all its own. The taboo alone was a dopamine hit.

The air smelled of dust and old glue. His flashlight beam danced across overturned desks, crumbling posters, and old bulletin boards still pinned with yellowing papers. There were faded murals on the wall, school spirit quotes, drawings of kids playing instruments or holding science beakers. The place felt like a time capsule... or a memory someone forgot to finish.

I wonder when the last time someone was in here.

There was a supply closet filled with VHS tapes and what looked like a bag of gym uniforms from 2007. A staircase led to the second floor with long-forgotten art rooms. In one of them, he found a broken pottery wheel and a row of student self-portraits, some still taped to the wall, their faces faded, their names written in blocky, middle-school handwriting. One was cute, and he wondered who she was.

He turned a corner and tripped over a loose board. His backpack hit the floor, and something bounced out of his jacket pocket — oh no, the padlock.

It slid across the cracked linoleum and slipped right into a floor vent, vanishing with a clink.

Alex scrambled after it and dropped to the floor, reaching into the narrow gap. He could see it about three feet down, but there was no way he could reach.

He stretched anyway, reaching, reaching... He felt a rush and then it moved. The lock floated.

It didn't roll or bounce. It lifted, as if someone was handing it to him from the other side.

He snatched it out of the air and sat there stunned, his breath fogging in the cold annex air. "What...?"

He looked around. There was no one. Nothing. Heart pounding, he placed the padlock gently on the floor in front of him. Alex took a deep breath.

"Okay," he whispered. "Try again."

He stared at it, reached his hand toward it like he was in a movie. Nothing happened.

He narrowed his focus. Reached again, not just with his fingers, but with that deep feeling you get when you feel a rush of adrenaline. A kind of pull. Like his hand was a magnet, and it rose.

The padlock hovered again, slightly shakier this time, but still, floating.

Alex let out a breathless laugh. "Oh my god, I've got to tell someone."

At that moment, he was pissed that no one was there to witness it . They were not going to believe him. Skeptical Lucas would have to see it; Hudson would say he believed but he wouldn't fully; Rachelle would believe but it would be her unconditional belief in him regardless of whether or not she truly believed.

He didn't know how. He didn't know why. But he could do it. He could lift things without touching them. He stood up, heart racing, eyes wide.

He grabbed his flashlight, stepped out of the annex, and wrapped the chain tightly back around the handles. He put the original lock in his backpack. The new padlock clicked into place with a satisfying snap. He ran to find the group, in such a hurry he never saw the dark figure standing in a dark corner of the main hall.

This time, the mystery was his.

He found the others by their lockers. Rachelle was there, looking tired but glad to be out of the house.

"Hey," she said, noticing his expression immediately. "You okay?"

"I went in."

Lucas perked up. "Into the annex? You're joking?"

Alex nodded, practically vibrating with excitement. "I saw everything. It's like a frozen time bubble in there. But that's not the crazy part."

He looked at each of them.

"I can... do something. I think I have powers or something. I made the padlock float. It was incredible."

Lucas blinked. "Wait... hold on, you did what?"

"I dropped it, and it came back to my hand. Then I did it again on purpose. Like, levitation. Telekinesis. I'm serious."

Hudson raised an eyebrow. "Dude. You get four hours of sleep, break into a sealed-off building, and now you think you're Eleven from that one show?"

"I'm not making it up!"

Lucas gave a skeptical shrug, setting his water bottle on the ground. "Okay. Show us, then."

Alex tried. He focused on his water bottle. Nothing. Focused harder. Still nothing.

"You look ridiculous," Lucas noted.

Hudson gave a flat look. "Yeah, alright. Guess it wore off. You must be out of your levitation fuel."

Lucas snorted. "Try caffeine next time."

They walked off toward class, still chuckling. Alex stared at his hands, frustrated. He didn't imagine it. He knew what he had seen. Rachelle stayed behind with him.

"You believe me, right?" he asked quietly

She didn't answer right away. But she didn't laugh either.

"I don't know what to think," she said finally. "But I don't think you're lying."

Alex nodded slowly. That was enough. For now.

"Thank you," he said.

He didn't know what he did to deserve Rachelle, but moments like this reminded him how much he valued her.

SOCIAL STUDIES AGAIN. Mr. Willy was mid-rant about the Mongol Empire, pointing at a map that looked like it had been printed before the internet existed. Alex sat at his desk, trying to focus, but his mind was still stuck on what had happened that morning.

The lock had floated.

But now, no matter how hard he tried, it wouldn't work again. He'd spent all morning holding pencils, paperclips, erasers, but nothing happened. Just sweat and frustration.

He glanced across the room at Hudson, who caught his eye and immediately held up his pen as if it was floating. He wiggled his fingers, exaggeratedly concentrating, then pretended the pen was flying away and smacked himself in the face with it.

Lucas saw and doubled over in silent laughter.

Alex narrowed his eyes and gave Hudson a lazy thumbs-up, their old signal for 'you're hilarious, please keep talking.' It was not sincere.

Lucas chimed in with his own performance, holding his notebook above the desk and pretending it was lifting by the power of his mind. Then he dropped it with a loud thud.

Mr. Willy looked up, frowning. "Lucas?"

"Sorry," Lucas said, deadpan. "Just experimenting with gravity."

Mr. Willy stared at Alex as if he knew something. "You seem different today, Alex."

Alex slouched lower in his seat, cheeks burning. He reached for his water bottle, flicked his fingers in the exact way he had that morning.

Nothing.

In front of him, Rachelle made eye contact with him and subtly tapped her pencil twice, then traced a quick circle on her desk — their symbol for **"I believe you."**

He gave a small nod back.

Then she added another signal. She held up her hand and curled the middle two fingers. That one meant I'm with you. It wasn't official; they made it up in 5th grade when her dog died and she couldn't talk in class. It had become their way of saying what didn't need to be said out loud.

Lucas raised an eyebrow when he caught that one. He made a dramatic gagging motion and mimed a heart exploding in his chest.

Alex shot him a glare and rolled his eyes. That wasn't a sign, just Lucas being dumb, but inwardly... he felt steadier. He and Rachelle had always been there for each other.

Maybe he couldn't prove it yet. Maybe Hudson and Lucas were going to keep making fun of him until they got bored. But Rachelle wasn't laughing. Somehow, that made all the difference.

Mr. Willy cleared his throat. "Alright, group work again. And this time, try not to weaponize your school supplies."

Alex sighed and reached for his textbook, trying to set aside the impossible secret he carried.

As Mr. Willy went on about trade routes and tax systems, Alex found his gaze drifting again, this time without meaning to.

Charlotte sat near the front, one row over, scribbling notes in the margins of her worksheet. Her handwriting was neat, loopy, almost artistic. She had drawn a cute anime character with a magic aura around them. She paused mid-sentence, glanced up... and looked right at him.

Alex froze.

She didn't look away. Instead, Charlotte tilted her head slightly, a small, curious smile tugging at her lips, genuine, not mocking. Her eyes sparkled like she was in on some joke only she knew. She saw her friend Amanda looking at her, so she played it off.

Then she turned back to her paper, like it was nothing.

But to Alex, it was everything. But she was the one who'd drawn the magical figure. She would surely be impressed if she found out Alex could do magic. He tried to focus, but it was hopeless.

For a brief, dizzy second, his entire world stopped spinning. No more floating padlocks. No more Lucas making air quotes. No more frustration about powers that wouldn't cooperate. Just her smile — small, perfect, and directed at him.

When the bell rang a few minutes later, he was still recovering. He couldn't get her out of his head.

After the end of the second period bell, the group met up at their lockers. The hallway buzzed with the usual between-class chaos. Backpacks swung like wrecking balls. Someone dropped a clarinet case. A couple of kids were loudly debating whether strawberry milk was a war crime.

Lucas leaned against his locker, holding his phone over his head like it was a trophy.

"Check out my robot's arm. It's almost done. It can pick up a can of soda and crush it like a movie villain." Lucas's grin stretched wide as he puffed out his chest.

Hudson nodded, impressed. "Sweet. Let's upgrade it to write our homework next."

"I'm thinking lasers are the next upgrade." Lucas proposed.

"Always go with the lasers." Hudson concurred.

Alex and Rachelle exchanged a glance, quietly amused. "You okay?" she asked him quietly.

"Yeah," Alex said. "Just, uh… Charlotte smiled at me. So I'm basically living in a music video right now."

Rachelle smirked. "Do I need to start snapping my fingers in slow motion while you walk down the hallway?"

"If you could do it with wind in my hair, that'd be great."

She rolled her eyes but laughed.

Lucas and Hudson peeled off when the warning bell rang, promising to reconvene for lunch to "test robot hand related theories." Once they were out of earshot, Alex turned to Rachelle, more serious now.

"Hey," he said. "About tomorrow morning…"

She raised an eyebrow. "Let me guess. You want to go back in."

"I have to," he said. "I know I sounded crazy earlier, but something happened in there, Rach. I felt it. I did something. And I think... I think I can do more."

She was quiet for a moment. Then she nodded. "Alright. I'll come with you."

"You sure?"

"I believe you, remember? Even if I don't totally get it yet."

Alex smiled, grateful. "We'll meet at the gates. Six? Bring a flashlight."

"And snacks," she added automatically.

"That's a given."

They bumped fists, their old tradition.

And as the hallway emptied around them, Alex felt that familiar thrum of excitement building in his chest again. This time, he wouldn't be alone. And maybe tomorrow, he'd finally figure out what he was becoming.

Third period was Intro to Graphic Design, and Alex sat in the second row, surrounded by kids he barely knew. The room buzzed with the soft clatter of keyboards and the low whir of old iMacs struggling to keep up with modern software.

Mr. Klinger was explaining the basics of layering and transparency masks, but Alex was only catching every fifth word. His screen was blank. His cursor blinked patiently. His mind was elsewhere.

He could still feel it — that moment, the weightless

rush when the lock had lifted into his hand. He hadn't imagined it. It had felt real. Like gravity had taken a coffee break and left him in charge.

He opened his backpack just a little and peered inside. The padlock was there, tucked in the front pocket. Inert. Normal. Not hovering. Not humming with alien energy. He took a moment to muse about how smart it had been to replace the lock. He didn't have to worry about picking it. He had a key.

He reached out a hand under the desk, palm open, just beneath the pocket. Nothing. No buzz. No twitch. No levitation.

Maybe it was the environment, he thought. Maybe something about the annex activated it. Or maybe it only worked when he was panicking. Which... didn't exactly narrow things down.

His fingers curled into a fist. He sighed.

Then, without warning, his mind swung hard in the other direction, straight to Charlotte.

The way she'd smiled at him. Not a smirk. Not a pity look. A real smile. Like she'd been curious. Maybe even... interested?

Nope, don't start with that, he told himself. *You floated a lock this morning, and your brain melted. That smile could've meant anything.*

But the smile wouldn't leave his head. Her expression had landed in the same place his mysterious powers had, right in the middle of his chest, like something glowing faintly from the inside out. She really was beautiful.

He stared at the blinking cursor again.

What if the two things were connected?

He chuckled softly at the thought. *Yeah, Alex. You get your first superpower, and the universe rewards you with attention from a girl you've never spoken to. It makes perfect sense.*

The kid next to him glanced over. "You good, dude?"

Alex blinked. "Huh? Oh—yeah. Sorry. Just... designing mentally."

The other kid nodded as if that made sense. Mr. Klinger was still talking about negative space.

Alex tried to concentrate, but his thoughts kept swinging back and forth like a pendulum: Powers. Charlotte. Powers. Charlotte. Powers. Charlotte.

A lock that floated. A smile that made his stomach flip.

And somehow, he was starting to believe that both of them, impossible as they were, might actually be real. They were real, they both happened, so why was that so hard to accept?

The hallways were chaos, backpacks swinging, lunch trays clattering, a kid yelling something about pizza pockets like it was life or death. Alex moved through it all with Lucas, Hudson, and Rachelle, heading toward the cafeteria. The four of them weaved through the crowd like a loose flock, half-joking, half-hungry.

"I swear," Hudson said, dodging a basketball that rolled past, "this school turns into a jungle at lunch. Like someone hits a button and all rules evaporate."

Lucas tossed a grape from his lunchbox into the air and caught it in his mouth. "It's controlled chaos. Darwin would be proud."

"There wouldn't be any finches left to study among this chaos," Hudson stated.

Lucas marveled at Hudson, That was an incredibly astute observation.

Rachelle was scrolling through her phone, half-listening, until she glanced up and nudged Alex. "Heads up. Your girl's incoming."

Alex followed her gaze, and there she was.

Charlotte.

The hallway seemed to bend slightly around her, the way it does when someone too cool walks through a scene you don't quite belong in. Her perfect blonde hair was tucked behind one ear, her hoodie perfectly over-sized like it had been selected by a stylist, not pulled from a pile. She had a sketchbook clutched to her chest and a wireless earbud in. She walked with easy confidence, graceful, but not showy. Like she didn't need to try. She just was.

Her eyes scanned the hallway casually, and then, somehow, they locked with Alex's. For a second, he thought he was imagining it. But no. She smiled.

"Hey, Alex," she said, her voice smooth and effortless, like they'd spoken a dozen times before.

He blinked. "Uh—hi."

His voice cracked halfway through the word. He tried to play it cool, but his face was probably a solid shade of firetruck red.

She kept walking, turning the corner behind him, the scent of her shampoo, coconut? Lingering like a gentle echo. His mind had left imagining her on a beach.

Alex turned to his friends, trying to look normal.

Lucas was gaping. "She knows your name?"

Hudson slapped him on the back. "Okay, okay, my guy!"

Rachelle just gave him a sideways look, one brow raised. "Not bad, Lockboy."

Alex grinned, dazed. "Did that just happen?"

"Oh, it happened," Lucas said, shaking his head. "This is a moment. You should commemorate it with a plaque or something."

"She said my name," Alex muttered, almost to himself.

They kept walking, the cafeteria doors in sight, but

everything else felt like background noise. The annex could wait. The mystery could wait.

For now, Charlotte said hi to him in the hallway.

And that was enough to carry him through the rest of the day.

Rachelle frowned. Some seventh graders were at their lunch table. "Nope, this is our table."

They started to protest until they saw Hudson.

Rachelle gave a subtle laugh. "It's a good thing they don't know what a gentle giant you are."

Hudson shrugged as they claimed their table. They loved this table tucked in the corner of the lunch area. Private and strategic, they could see the whole area.

THE ANNEX CALLS

Alex had been waiting at the gate for fifteen minutes, rocking on his heels, buzzing with nervous energy, watching every car that rolled up. His breath hung in the cold morning air, and it was just starting to lighten into a steel-gray dawn.

He checked his phone again. No new messages. Then he saw her. Rachelle hopped out of her brother's car, hoodie zipped high, hands shoved deep in her sleeves. She had her hair tied back, but a few strands had fallen loose and caught the wind as she jogged toward him. And for some reason, maybe the light, or maybe just the fact that they were meeting like this, alone, before the world woke up, Alex thought: *She's prettier than I remembered.*

Not in some dramatic, music-video kind of way.

Just... sharper. Brighter. Like his brain was seeing her differently now.

He looked away before she got too close.

"You look like a raccoon who found energy drinks," she said, eyeing the bags under his eyes.

"I slept for two hours," Alex said. "Couldn't stop thinking about today."

"I hope that was about floating locks and not Charlotte."

He gave her a weak grin. "Mostly locks."

They didn't say much as they crept through the school. The halls were still and quiet in that eerie early-morning way, lit only by the faint red glow of exit signs and the pale light filtering through the high windows. It felt like they were trespassing in time.

"You ready for this?" he asked at the chained double doors of the annex.

Rachelle gave a shrug that tried to be casual but didn't quite reach her eyes. "As I'll ever be."

He knelt, put his key in the lock. Keys were definitely faster than picking. It popped open with a satisfying click. He pulled the chain free, pocketed the lock, and they slipped inside.

The air changed instantly. Colder. Heavier. Still.

They wandered deeper than he had gone yesterday. Through quiet, dust-choked halls. Past empty classrooms frozen in time. The place felt more alive with someone else there, more real. But also more dangerous.

Rachelle ran her hand across a faded mural of students holding hands. "This place is like a ghost story."

Alex led her to the commons area — open, wide, quiet. Debris littered the floor. The light came in slanted through dirty windows, hazy and soft.

"Watch your step; there is stuff all over the floor," he pointed out.

Once she was settled in a clear spot, he said, "Okay. Watch this."

He knelt, gathered a few small stones in his palm, then stepped back. He took a deep breath. He tried to remember how it felt. Focus. Feel. Pull.

The stones lifted, slowly at first, then faster, spiraling above their heads, spinning into motion like a flock of birds caught in a current. They twisted and arched, weaving around each other in perfect patterns, folding and blooming like a living fractal. They made no sound but filled the air with motion and shape and wonder.

Rachelle stared up at them, her lips slightly parted. The rocks slowed, then drifted back to the ground with soft, hollow taps.

Alex looked at her, heart pounding. "So...?"

She nodded slowly. "Okay. That was... something."

"Have you tried anything bigger?"

Alex scrunched up his face. "I was kind of freaked last time."

He focused on a cinder block. Up it went, no tricky maneuvers, just proof he could move bigger objects. He lowered it down with a clunk.

She dropped her backpack and sat cross-legged on the floor. "Alright. My turn."

Alex gave her space. "Just... try to feel it. Don't overthink."

She stared at a rock. Focused. Nothing happened. Again. Again. Over and over. She gritted her teeth.

"Okay, I'm officially feeling nothing," she muttered. "Like, less than nothing. I feel negative progress."

Alex raised his hands. "It's okay. Maybe it's different for you."

"Oh great, I'm defective," she snapped, standing.

"No, I didn't mean..." He tried to explain.

"I know what you meant," she said too quickly. "I just..."

She clenched her fists, her face flushed. Then, without warning, she shouted in frustration and threw her hands down at her sides.

Little balls of fire rolled around in her palms, bright and wild. Startled, she whipped her hands trying to put them out. She screamed and flapped her hands, sending little firebolts flinging off. To avoid getting burnt, Alex jumped behind a pile of cinder blocks that had been a wall at some point.

Alex stared, eyes wide. "Whoa! Whoa."

Rachelle calmed herself, breathing hard, staring at her own hand. "I didn't mean to; I didn't even think..."

He took a step closer cautiously. "Rach... you just made fire."

She looked at him, her eyes wide and unsteady. "I couldn't move a pebble. But I can do that?"

Alex nodded slowly. "Yeah. Looks like it."

They stood in stunned silence for a moment, the scent of scorched metal still hanging in the air.

"I didn't think about that; you know there could be other powers," Alex said finally, a smile tugging at the edge of his mouth.

She exhaled, still shaken. "I didn't think I'd be able to do anything."

Their eyes met again, and this time, something unspoken sat between them, new and complicated. They held the look, not sure if it was just the secret they now shared or something else.

They didn't know what they were stepping into. Or what it meant. But they were in it now. Alex was excited to have someone to share it with.

They stayed in the annex until the light coming through the grimy windows turned gold, ticking down the minutes until first period. Neither said much at first. They didn't need to.

Rachelle stood in the open space where Alex had done his rock dance earlier. Her hoodie was tied around her waist now, sleeves rolled up to her elbows. Her stance was wide, stable, and intentional.

Alex watched her with a quiet mix of awe and something else he didn't want to name yet.

She held her hand out, took a breath, and willed the fire forward. A flicker sparked in her palm. Then another. It grew into a flame the size of a tennis ball, glowing orange and gold like a captured sun.

She didn't flinch.

With a fluid motion, she tossed it across the room. It arced high, hit a hanging ceiling tile, and vanished into smoke.

"Again," she said, resetting her stance.

Another flame. This one spun slightly in her palm before she released it, faster and straighter.

Then a third. This time she whipped her arm as if she was throwing a lasso, and the fire trailed behind it in a long ribbon, curling and cracking through the air before snapping out like a whip against the far wall.

Alex jumped.

She turned back to him, breathing hard, grinning.

"That looked like a weapon," he said quietly.

Rachelle didn't answer right away. She just stared at

her hand, watching the tiny flickers dance across her fingers before they vanished.

"I don't know what this is," she said. "But I can feel it. Like it's just... waiting to come out. It doesn't feel unnatural. It feels like I've always had it, and just forgot."

Alex looked at the scattered rocks on the floor. "Mine's different. Lighter. More... delicate, I guess."

"You have control," she said. "I have chaos."

She wasn't bragging. But there was something in her voice, an edge of pride. Or defiance. He didn't know how to respond to that.

Rachelle raised both hands now. A sphere of flame grew between them, swirling and pulsing with light. It floated just above her palms, spinning slightly, contained, for now.

"You're picking it up really fast," Alex said.

She smiled faintly. "I don't think I have a choice."

She snapped her hands apart. The fireball burst into embers, scattering like tiny sparks before dissolving.

They stood there for a few long seconds, both breathing harder than they should have been.

Then Rachelle finally said, "We're not normal anymore, are we?"

Alex shook his head. "Not even close."

She bent down to grab her backpack. "We should go. The halls are going to start filling up."

Alex lingered for a second, staring at the scorch marks on the walls, the faint heat still clinging to the air. He thought back to that morning's excitement, when it was his secret. His discovery. His moment. Now? Rachelle had fire dancing in her hands, and he suddenly wasn't sure where this was all going. But this time they had to believe. He scooped up a charred piece of a locker tag.

As they locked the annex doors behind them and slipped back into the waking school, the air between them carried something new: wonder, fear. And a power neither of them fully understood.

Alex and Rachelle joined Lucas and Hudson by the lockers just before first period, like they always did. Kids flowed past in noisy, half-awake clumps, but Alex barely noticed. His heart was pounding again, different from yesterday's Charlotte-induced flutter. This was the please-don't-think-I'm-insane kind.

Lucas took one look at Alex's face and raised an eyebrow. "Alright, spill. You guys were definitely up to something."

Rachelle crossed her arms, nodding slightly. "We went back into the annex this morning."

"Of course you did," Hudson said with a snort.

"What'd you do this time? Channel the ghosts of forgotten lunch ladies?"

"Actually," Alex said, glancing around and lowering his voice, "we figured out what's going on with us."

Lucas rolled his eyes. "Oh, here we go..."

"I moved things, okay? With my mind. And Rachelle..."

"I can conjure fire," she shouted, as if it were just a fact now.

Lucas blinked. "You mean like... fire, fire?"

Rachelle didn't smile. "I can throw it. We spent an hour practicing. Ask Alex."

"Okay, now you're just trying to impress me," Hudson said. But his smirk faded a little when he caught the look in her eyes.

Lucas looked back and forth between them. "So... you two are both taking drugs? It's the most logical explanation. "

Rachelle gave Lucas a shove.

Alex chuckled to himself. Fire made so much sense for Rachelle.

"You think I'd wake up at six AM to help Alex sell a lie?" Rachelle asked.

Lucas gave a skeptical shrug. "I mean, it is Alex."

"Dude," Hudson said, eyes narrowing. "You know you would do anything for Alex?"

Alex sighed and opened his bag, revealing the

scorched locker tag he picked up in the annex, still blackened from Rachelle's flames.

"That wasn't there yesterday," Alex said. "And I sure didn't burn it."

The bell rang, interrupting them. Students started filing into Mr. Willy's social studies class, and their group broke apart with the crowd. Hudson and Lucas were still whispering as they sat, but the conversation wasn't over. Not even close.

Mr. Willy launched into his daily routine with gusto: a lecture about empires rising and falling, illustrated with a hand-drawn cartoon of a lion and a crumbling castle. Alex sat two rows across from Lucas, and Hudson was on the opposite side. Rachelle was two seats in front of him. They caught his eye immediately.

Lucas scratched his chin, then tapped the top of his desk twice. **"You serious?"** The signal was simple but pointed.

Alex glanced down, made a slow clockwise circle with his pen. **"Swear."**

Hudson made the whoa face, then mimed something rising with his hands. **"How?"**

Alex gave a small shrug. **"No clue. It just happens."**

Then Lucas grinned and held up his hands dramatically, miming fire shooting from his fingers. Alex narrowed his eyes and flipped his pen toward Rachelle. **"Not me. Her."**

Rachelle glanced over and caught the motion. She gave them a small, private nod. Then, just to show off, she traced a figure-eight motion on her desk — their old signal for **"believe it."**

Hudson dropped his head onto the desk in silent disbelief.

Mr. Willy turned suddenly mid-sentence. "Something funny about Hammurabi's Code, Mr. Jeffries?"

Hudson sat bolt upright. "No sir. Just... amazed at the legal innovations."

Lucas snort-laughed into his sleeve.

Alex sat back in his chair, adrenaline fading into something steadier. The secret was out, sort of. And even though Lucas and Hudson weren't totally convinced yet, they were interested. That was enough. For now. But it wouldn't be long before they'd need to see it for themselves. And when they did, everything would change.

The signal language was flying fast now. Lucas pantomimed a mini fireball soaring over a notebook. Hudson responded with a series of exaggerated "mind push" gestures that ended with him pretending to fall out of his chair.

Alex barely suppressed a laugh, his shoulders twitching as he mimed flicking a pebble into orbit. Across the room, Rachelle caught it and replied with a tiny flame-symbol drawn on the edge of her desk in pencil. Just a spark sketch, but Alex saw it, and it made his chest warm.

He didn't notice Charlotte.

But she was noticing him, and the energy in his friend group. Something was up. She had overheard bits and pieces, but nothing definitive, not yet. She sat three seats to his left, diagonally across from him. Her sketchbook was open, but the pencil resting between her fingers hadn't moved in minutes. Instead, her eyes were on Alex.

She had noticed the signals. She didn't know what they meant, but that there was something, something quick and lively and secret, happening between him and his friends. The way his expression changed. The way he smiled at Rachelle's little flame drawing.

The way he didn't look her way. Not even once. Charlotte stared at him for a long moment, something unreadable in her expression. Curious, maybe. Or thoughtful. Or... disappointed.

Then she blinked, looked back down at her sketchbook, and finally turned her body toward the front of the room. Mr. Willy's voice filtered back in, dry as dust.

"Now, what can we learn from the fall of Mesopotamia? Anyone?" Mr. Willy asked again.

Charlotte stared off at nothing for a long moment, then turned back to her sketchbook. Her pencil moved slowly, carefully. A dark hallway. A chained door. A figure with a stone in his hand. Just a sketch. But not a random one. She notices more than Alex realized.

And Alex? He didn't even realize she'd been watching.

After second period, they convened their meeting at the lockers. They had barely started talking when Charlotte walked up.

"Alex, can I talk to you?" She motioned for him to follow.

"Hi" he said, not sure what else to say.

"Can you teach me the signals?" She bit her lower lip.

Girl sorcery — they all seem to know how to do it, simple gestures to get their way.

"Umm... I would if it was up to me, but it's a group arrangement, so we would have to talk and vote on it." Alex looked down, then looked back at her.

"We'll talk, and I'll let you know," Alex said. She was watching him closely, not smiling this time. Just... waiting. And he wasn't sure if he wanted her to be part of the secret, or if it had ever been just his to share. "I'll find you in the library after school," Alex said.

The hallway between second and third period buzzed with the usual chaos, lockers slamming, sneakers squeaking, overlapping voices rising and falling like an off-key chorus. But at the far end, just past the art wing where the noise thinned out, four friends huddled closer than usual.

Alex leaned back against the cool metal of locker 216, arms crossed, trying to read the room before he said anything. Rachelle was already giving him that look, the one that said she knew he was hiding something. Lucas bounced on his toes like he couldn't wait to speak, and Hudson had one AirPod dangling like he'd been caught halfway through a bass drop.

"Okay," Alex said finally. "She asked."

Lucas straightened. "Charlotte?"

Alex nodded. "She wants to learn the signals."

Lucas let out a low whistle. "No way. Dude, that's... that's big."

Hudson grinned. "Cosmic, even. Charlotte, joining us? That's like... main character energy."

Rachelle's arms folded tighter across her chest. "It's not a game, you guys."

The smile faded from Hudson's face. "Didn't say it was."

"We invented that signal language before anything weird even happened," she went on. "Back when it was just something fun. But now? Now it's practically a security system. You want to hand her the keys to the vault?"

"She just wants to learn the basics," Alex said gently. "Not... all of it."

Lucas made a face. "I mean, what's the risk, really? She learns a few silent cues, some hand flicks. It's not like we're giving her a spellbook."

"Right," Hudson added. "Unless the signal for 'Alex is floating lunch trays again' is in there."

Rachelle shot them both a hard look. "It's never just the basics. You start with hello and goodbye, and then suddenly she's catching on to the ones we use during higher stakes. Or about the annex. Or when one of us... is in trouble."

Alex winced. He still remembered Rachelle's scorched locker door from this morning. So did she.

Lucas tried again. "Look, Charlotte's sharp. She's already picking up on stuff. I saw her watching us during the science lab; she's not dumb. We shut her out now; it'll just make her more suspicious."

"And suspicious people dig," Hudson said, nodding. "Sometimes it's better to bring someone into the tent than leave them looking in through the flaps."

Rachelle's eyes flicked toward Alex. "You trust her because you like her."

Alex blinked, caught off guard. "That's not... okay, maybe. But it's not just that. She's kind. She listens. She's not the type to blow things up for attention."

"That's ironic, coming from us," Lucas muttered, though he held up a hand when Rachelle glared. "Sorry. Just saying."

"I don't want her to feel left out," Alex said, quieter now. "But we can't pretend this is some secret club anymore. We're not making decoder rings; we're dealing with real stuff. The annex. Whatever's down there. If we bring her in, even a little, we need to be sure."

A pause settled over them. Someone's locker slammed shut down the hall, the echo bouncing into their silence.

Hudson broke it first. "What if we compromise? Teach her the signal language, but only the safe ones. No codewords for powers. Nothing about the annex. Just the surface level."

"Like a trial membership," Lucas added. "She gets the handshake, not the vault passcode."

"She will notice," Rachelle said. "She'll ask why some signals are off-limits."

"Then we'll be vague," Alex said. "We say it's private. Personal. And if she presses harder, if she gets too close to what we're hiding, we talk about it. Together. No secrets between each other. Deal?"

Rachelle looked at each of them. Lucas, Hudson, Alex. "You're all really into this, huh?"

"She's already on the edge of it," Alex said, voice calm. "We're just deciding whether to build her a bridge or leave her outside in the dark."

Another pause. Then Rachelle sighed, long and low.

"Fine," she said. "Teach her the basics. But if she even hints that she knows more than she should — one weird comment about fire or floating objects or dusty doors — we pull the plug. This is ours, and if it becomes a joke or is used against us, I may have to smash someone."

Alex nodded. "Deal."

"Deal," Lucas echoed.

Hudson gave a thumbs up. "Sweet."

The bell rang sharp and sudden. Students spilled back into the hallway like a shaken ant farm. As the group drifted apart, Alex felt the knot in his chest loosen slightly. He had no idea what Charlotte would do with what they gave her, but at least now, they'd face it together.

The library after school was nearly empty, save for the sound of a distant cart squeaking and the soft buzz of fluorescent lights. Outside the tall windows, storm clouds gathered in slow coils. Thundercloud gray.

Charlotte sat at one of the study tables near the back, her backpack half-unzipped and a paperback flipped open but unread. She looked up the moment Alex and Rachelle stepped around the bookshelf.

"You came," she said, voice soft but steady.

Alex gave a small smile. "Told you we would."

Rachelle stayed standing while Alex slid into the seat across from Charlotte. Her arms were crossed, her stance stiff, like she wasn't ready to sit, or trust, just yet.

Charlotte looked between them. "So... what was the consensus?"

Rachelle arched a brow. "You're observant; you know more than you say."

Charlotte didn't flinch. "It's hard not to notice when you and your friends start using a silent language in front of me. Especially during weird moments."

Alex cleared his throat. "Okay, look. You're right. We do use signals. And... we've kept it secret on purpose."

Charlotte straightened. "Because it's something unique to you?"

Rachelle shot Alex a look, but he spoke first. "Yes, it's ours. It's personal. It started long ago as something fun between friends. But it's become more than that."

Charlotte tilted her head. "Like... spy stuff?"

"Not even close," Rachelle cut in, voice sharp. "This isn't some code-breaking club or a prank squad. What we're letting you in on, it's private. And important to us."

Charlotte held Rachelle's gaze without blinking. "I'm not trying to mess anything up. I just... I like you guys. You're way more interesting than everyone else. I want in, not just on the side watching. When I moved here, Amanda latched on to me, but just because of the way I look."

Alex smiled a little at that. Rachelle didn't.

"We're going to teach you some of the signals," Rachelle said. "Not all. Just the basics. The ones we use at school, or in public when we can't talk."

Charlotte's brows lifted. "So there are secret ones?"

Rachelle's expression turned to stone. "You don't get to ask about those, not yet."

There was a beat of silence. Charlotte nodded. "Ok I understand."

"You don't repeat them," Rachelle continued. "Not to your sister. Not to your best friend. Not to anyone. Not even as a joke. If someone outside this group ever mimics one of our signals, it could... cause a problem. A big one."

Charlotte blinked. "I wouldn't."

"You'd better not," Rachelle said.

Alex stepped in, his voice softer. "Rachelle's not trying to scare you. We just need you to be careful. We're trusting you, Charlotte. And trust isn't something we hand out a lot."

Charlotte nodded again, slower this time. "I get it. I do."

Rachelle still hadn't sat down. Her eyes stayed locked on Charlotte, measuring her, weighing every word.

"Once you're in," Rachelle said, "you're in. That means you don't run your mouth. And you don't disappear when things get weird. Because they will get weird."

Charlotte's lips parted, half nervous, half excited. "That sounds promising."

Rachelle finally allowed herself the smallest of smirks. "It's a warning."

Alex exhaled and reached into his backpack, pulling out a folded sheet of lined paper. He handed it to Charlotte.

"This is a starter guide," he said. "A dozen or so signals. Simple stuff, 'yes,' 'no,' 'trouble,' 'split up,' and a few others."

Charlotte unfolded the paper with care, eyes scanning the symbols like she was decoding a treasure map. "Do I get a test?"

Rachelle snorted. "If you mess up in the real world, that's the test."

"I won't," Charlotte said, folding the paper again. "Thanks. For trusting me."

Alex smiled again. "Let's see how you do first."

And finally, Rachelle slid into the chair beside him. "Don't, let us down"

Charlotte locked eyes with Rachelle.

"I've got this, watch and see. Your group reminds me

of the friends I had to leave when we moved. It's nice to connect, you remind me of them."

4

ROCKS AND FIREBALLS

The morning was still when Alex and Rachelle slipped through the narrow gap in the gate and vanished into the school's forgotten service corridor. Mist clung to the concrete like memory, curling around their ankles as they walked. Their sneakers barely made a whisper against the cool, dusty tile. Above them, fluorescent lights buzzed faintly, some flickering weakly, others dead-eyed and silent, casting the hallway in a patchwork of shifting shadows.

The air smelled of old copper and mildew, like something long buried trying to breathe again.

"Feels different today," Rachelle murmured, her voice barely audible, like it didn't want to wake the walls. She glanced warily upward at the stained drop-ceiling tiles, where sections sagged like bruised skin and the light danced in nervous spasms.

Alex nodded, jaw tight, pulse thudding louder than their footsteps. "Yeah," he said after a long breath. "Like it knows we're back."

They stopped before the double doors at the end of the hall. They loomed tall, metal, dented, and veined with rust, like a cage locking away some slumbering horror. A beat passed in silence as they looked at each other, uncertainty swimming just behind their eyes. Then, Alex reached out. The cold handle bit into his palm. The hinges gave a groaning whisper, as though trying to warn them.

Beyond the Annex lay in wait.

Crossing the threshold was like stepping into a different world. The air grew heavy and humid, thick with a strange warmth that pressed against their skin like invisible hands. It smelled faintly of burnt herbs and old stone. The floor creaked softly beneath them, even though it was concrete.

They moved quietly, exploring further than they'd dared before. Past the ancient, rust-streaked boilers that exhaled metallic sighs, past dented lockers scarred with graffiti in languages they didn't recognize. Past a crooked stairwell and a door with a cracked mirror that didn't quite reflect what it should.

The space they entered yawned open like a

forgotten mouth, too large for a classroom, too strange for a gym. It wasn't a theater, but stage lights hung high above like waiting eyes, and the floor was pocked with old painted lines and stage markings. The ceiling only half-existed, crumbling in parts to reveal pipes and blackness beyond, as if the building had given up pretending it knew what this room had been for.

Alex stopped in the center, heart racing. "This place..." he said, voice soft and awed.

Rachelle was staring at the wall, her arms crossed, fingertips ghosting over a patch of scorched paint. "It remembers," she whispered. "I swear it remembers us."

Their breath fogged faintly in the space, even though it was warm. It clung to the light and made halos around every shadow.

Rachelle dropped her backpack and glanced at him. "Are you sure you want to try this?"

Alex nodded, already stretching his fingers. "We've been practicing small stuff. Time to level up."

"Right," she said, drawing in a breath and planting her feet. "Just don't... slam me into a wall."

Alex gave a crooked grin. "You saying you don't trust me?"

"I'm saying I like my bones unbroken."

He closed his eyes and focused, the way he always did when the air around him felt just barely touchable. His palms lifted slightly, fingers trembling.

He was nervous; he didn't want to see her hurt, so he held his focus more than before.

Rachelle rose. Slowly at first. Her sneakers left the floor by inches, then a foot, then two. Her arms splayed for balance, her eyes wide, not in fear exactly, but in the white-knuckle awareness of someone stepping off a ledge.

"You're okay," Alex said. "You're weightless. I've got you."

She floated forward, smooth and slow, as if she was gliding underwater. Her hair drifted slightly in the still air.

Then she let out a laugh, sharp and surprised. "This is insane."

Alex grinned. "You look like a superhero."

"I feel like a balloon."

"A pretty balloon," he said before he had time to think, but now it was out there.

He lowered her gently, carefully, but her feet thudded onto the floor harder than he intended.

"Sorry." He grimaced.

When she stumbled and steadied herself, she turned in a tight circle, then smacked him on the arm. "Okay, your turn to help me."

Alex raised a brow. "You gonna try to launch me across the room?"

"Nope." She reached into her bag and pulled out a

tennis ball, handing it to Alex.

"Throw it," she said.

Alex threw it as hard as he could. She sent a dart of flame right through the ball. "Wow, that was amazing," Alex said with true admiration of her skill.

"What now?" he asked.

"I'm going to hit that exit sign. From here."

He turned to look. The sign was at least a hundred feet away, above a set of double doors, half-obscured by shadows. "You sure..."

Before he could finish, Rachelle raised her hand and let a fireball fly. It zipped through the air like a bullet and struck dead center of the plastic casing of the sign, causing it to melt and drip to the ground. Alex turned back, his jaw dropped.

She shrugged. "When I focus, I don't miss."

They stayed another half hour, pushing their limits. Alex lifted a broom across the room, turning it slowly midair like a compass needle. Rachelle ricocheted small bits of flame off the far walls, calling each target before she sent at it.

By the time they left, the school was just beginning to stir. As they walked out, she punched him in the arm.

"That's for calling me pretty when I was trying to focus," she said as she bit her lip.

Girl sorcery

They quickly found Lucas and Hudson by the

vending machines near the side entrance, sipping apple juice and talking about a video they saw, like it was any other Thursday.

Alex and Rachelle walked up, both flushed from the cold morning and whatever heat still clung to them from the Annex.

"You two look like you ran laps," Lucas said, eyeing them.

"It was amazing," Alex said. "And we want you to come with us."

Hudson perked up. "The Annex?"

Rachelle nodded. "You will never believe until you see it, so come see it."

Lucas narrowed his eyes. "How early?"

"Six a.m.," Alex said. "Before the teachers get in. Before the building wakes up."

Hudson grinned. "Sounds perfect. I'm down."

Lucas tapped his juice bottle. "This better not be a ghost."

Rachelle gave him a tight smile. "It's not a ghost. It's better."

They agreed to meet at the gate again, exactly at six the next morning.

As the first bell rang, the four of them split up and headed to class, but something had shifted. Not just in the air, but between them. A new alignment. A quiet charge. The kind of current that only flowed between people carrying the same secret.

Mr. Willy stood at the front of the room, half-turned to the class as he scribbled "Causes of the War of 1812" on the whiteboard. His plaid shirt was rumpled as usual, the sleeves rolled to the elbows, and his voice plodded through the lecture like a horse pulling a heavy cart.

Alex sat near the middle of the room, flipping his pencil in slow circles as he tuned in and out of phrases like "maritime trade routes" and "impressment of sailors." In front of him, Rachelle was sitting upright and quiet, eyes alert beneath her dark curls. Lucas was to the left of Alex, looking through a spiral notebook and half-heartedly pretending to care about historical grievances. Hudson to his right looked lost in a daydream.

And Charlotte, new to the group and eager to belong, was watching everything. She caught Alex's eye and gave a little tap with her knuckles: once, twice, three taps on her thigh and swiped her knee. It was slightly off-tempo, but Alex recognized the attempt. **"Bored out of my skull?"**

He raised an eyebrow, then gave a subtle nod. It was odd; the signal was right, but from a new person, it felt odd.

Charlotte pointed at the board, where Mr. Willy had

underlined "Trade Restrictions," then glanced dramatically at the classroom clock. With her hands below the desk, she tried a shaky version of their **"this is lame"** sign. It was awkward, but the effort was all there.

Rachelle noticed. Her mouth twitched like she was trying not to smile, but she gave an approving nod.

Charlotte lit up, encouraged. She tried another, a goofy, exaggerated yawn behind her hand: **"Make this end."**

Lucas caught it from the corner of his eye and snorted under his breath.

Hudson gave a quiet tap of fingers against his backpack: **"Nice."**

But Rachelle's face sobered. She glanced toward the right side of the room. Two desks over, Amanda was staring, not directly at them, but close enough. Her eyes flicked between Charlotte and Lucas.

That was enough.

Rachelle turned just slightly and signed to Charlotte with practiced sharpness. Two fingers to the shoulder, then a flat palm down: **"Stop."**

Charlotte blinked, confused for a beat.

Rachelle followed with a quick downward sweep: **"Lower. Subtle."**

She followed with a single tap to the nose: **"They are listening."**

Charlotte's eyes widened with realization. She nodded quickly. Then mouthed, "Sorry."

Alex watched it unfold, that fragile moment balanced between inclusion and secrecy. Charlotte was trying so hard, smart, fast, and clearly picking up signals they hadn't even formally taught her. But Rachelle was right. They couldn't afford the exposure.

Not after everything they'd already risked. Not with what they'd found beneath the school.

The room settled. Mr. Willy kept lecturing, blissfully unaware, now describing the failed invasion of Canada with too much enthusiasm.

Charlotte folded her hands on her desk. Her face was composed, but her eyes sparkled with something Alex recognized: belonging. Even muted, even restrained, she liked being part of the group. And if she'd learned anything today, it was this: the language wasn't just in the signals. It was in knowing when not to use them.

After class, Mr. Willy noticed Charlotte's notebook left on her desk. He looked at the pictures of magical characters and scowled.

The cafeteria buzzed with lunchtime noise, plastic trays clattering, sports teams shouting across tables, the hum of half a thousand conversations layered over each other. At their usual spot near the back wall, Alex,

Rachelle, Lucas, and Hudson sat close, heads slightly bowed.

Alex picked at a soggy pizza slice on his tray, still thinking about that fireball hitting the exit sign.

Rachelle was quiet too, her eyes narrowed as she scanned the room.

"Look across the cafeteria, in the opposite corner," she said suddenly. "Charlotte is with the plastics."

Lucas followed her gaze.

Charlotte sat among the glossy-haired, always-laughing crowd near the front corner of the room. Amanda was there too, whispering something behind her hand to another girl with highlighter-blue nails. Their eyes flicked toward Charlotte, then over to Alex's table.

"Amanda saw Charlotte signal to us", Rachelle stated. Charlotte wasn't laughing with them. She was sitting straight-backed, not saying much, pushing the peas on her tray into organized rows.

"She looks miserable," Hudson said.

"She should be," Rachelle muttered. "They're giving her the look."

Lucas frowned. "The look?"

"You know." Rachelle tilted her chin toward the other table. "The 'why-are-you-talking-to-the-weirdos' look."

"She's just trying to belong to both worlds," Hudson said.

"She doesn't get both," Rachelle snapped. "Not if she's throwing our signals around like a handshake in History class. You can't teach them to people like that."

"It was a mistake to let her in," Rachelle said.

Lucas nodded.

Alex looked up. "Come on, she's not one of them. She's... just figuring things out."

Rachelle's jaw tightened. "If those signals get passed around, if they end up as some dumb inside joke with the popular crowd, we lose everything. We lose our edge. We lose our safety. This isn't a game, Alex."

Lucas held up a hand. "Okay. But maybe don't bite her head off over it, alright? She didn't know what it was going to be like with the plastics."

"We should have known," Rachelle said. "She could have guessed, it would be like this."

Lucas looked at her hard. "You know how that group works. You show weakness, you're done. She was trying to keep her head down, and she still got heat for even talking to us. You saw it."

"I saw someone who wasn't loyal to us," Rachelle said. Her voice was cold.

Across the room, Charlotte stood abruptly. Amanda said something sharp as she passed, and Charlotte didn't even respond. She just walked away from the table and tossed her tray with a loud clang into the bin. Then she disappeared into the hallway.

Alex watched her go, his stomach twisting.

"She didn't look like someone who wants to laugh at us," Hudson said. "She looked like someone who doesn't know who she's allowed to be."

Rachelle said nothing. She stabbed a carrot with her fork as if it had personally offended her.

Lucas leaned back in his chair. "I'm going to wait and see; I don't know what I would do in her shoes."

Alex nodded slowly, eyes still on the doors Charlotte had walked through. He agreed with Lucas; she may still do right by them. But in the pit of his stomach, he feared Rachelle could be right.

In the last class of the day, the final bell was still twenty minutes away, but Alex was already checked out. His math teacher, Mr. Ervin, was deep into equations, projected up front in neat, chalk-dusted lines. The room was quiet except for the scratch of pencils and the hum of the overhead lights. Alex stared at his blank worksheet, then glanced toward the narrow window near the door.

That's when he saw her. Charlotte.

She stood in the hallway, peering in through the glass. Her long blonde hair was tucked behind her ears, her eyes wide and urgent. She made a small motion, her finger curling twice.

Alex blinked. His heart jumped. *What's this about?*

He raised his hand. "Mr. Ervin?"

Mr. Ervin didn't look up. "Yes, Alex?"

"I need to go to the bathroom."

Mr. Ervin paused before answering, "Can it wait ten minutes? We're reviewing for the quiz..."

"It's an emergency," Alex said a little too loudly, now everyone looked up.

Mr. Ervin sighed, waved toward the pass. "Fine. Take the blue one. Sign out."

Alex scribbled his name in the log and grabbed the grimy laminated pass. He pushed through the door and stepped into the hallway.

Charlotte was already walking away, but paused at the water fountain, waiting. When he caught up, she didn't speak. She just handed him a folded square of paper, eyes on the ground, and whispered, "Read it when you're alone."

Then she turned and bolted down the corridor, her footsteps soft but fast, disappearing around the corner without a glance back. Alex stood there for a moment, stunned. The hallway echoed emptily around him.

He ducked into the bathroom, locked himself in a stall, and unfolded the note. Her handwriting was neat, sharp-angled but careful.

Alex,

I'm sorry.

Today was a mess, and I made it worse.

I didn't stand up for you. Or Rachelle. Or the group.

I should've said something. But I didn't, because I was afraid. Afraid of being dropped, laughed at, shut out. I'm afraid of being ridiculed and of being "seen as cut off" in this school, and I think I'm not worthy of your group.

But you made me feel real. Like I wasn't just another perfect girl at the perfect table saying perfect things.

I should have stood up for myself and said I'll be friends with who I want to, but I failed. I'm not proud of that. I don't even know what to do now. I messed up the right choice. But I want to be honest with you.

I do like you. And I won't leak your signals or secrets. Not ever.

If you don't trust me after this, I get it. I just didn't want to leave it unsaid. Please don't hate me.

Charlotte

Alex read it twice. Then, a third time. His stomach was doing flips, not sure if it was anxiety or something else entirely. Charlotte Novikova had written him a note. A real one. With complicated, honest, messy feelings in it.

He stood in the bathroom for another minute, the paper soft in his hands, his mind louder than the hallway outside.

Later that afternoon, walking home with his hoodie pulled up, he texted Rachelle.

Alex:

Charlotte passed me a note in math.

I think you were right. But also…
maybe not totally.

She says she won't say anything.

She apologized for not sticking up
for us.

There was a long pause before the bubbles appeared.

Rachelle:

Hm.

That doesn't mean I trust her.

Alex stared at the screen before replying.

Alex:

I'm not sure I do either, not totally.

But I think she wants to be better.

I think she means it.

Another pause.

Rachelle:

Then we'll find out.

Alex locked his phone. When he got home, he tucked the note into his sketchbook, pressing it between two blank pages. He didn't know whether it meant something. Or everything.

Alex lay on his bed, staring at the ceiling, the glow of his desk lamp casting a soft yellow light across the posters on his wall, an old movie poster, a solar system chart, a crooked sketch Rachelle had drawn of a dinosaur wearing sunglasses. He smiled at how long they had been friends.

His math book was still open beside him, but he hadn't looked at it in twenty minutes.

Instead, he kept replaying the moment Rachelle

lifted into the air that morning. Her arms stretched out, hovering as if gravity had forgotten her. Then the heat from her fireball. The crisp, perfect arc as it tore through the air and melted the exit sign.

He turned the page of his notebook and started doodling — tiny orbits, little shapes rising like pebbles in flight. He could move things. Really move them. With his mind. He still didn't know how. Or why. Or what it meant. And Rachelle hadn't just gotten better with fire. She had mastered it in one day. Like it had always been waiting for her. He closed the notebook and lay back again, hands behind his head.

What if Lucas had something too? Something electric, maybe; he was always playing with gadgets, always sparking some weird device to life. It made sense.

And Hudson... Alex grinned to himself. Hudson would have something big. Something that hit hard, strength maybe. Or invulnerability. He was always the one who leapt into a situation without flinching.

He tried to imagine all four of them — the crew — down in the Annex together, discovering something bigger than just powers. A purpose. A mission. Some kind of reason this was all happening to them.

But then his thoughts drifted inevitably to Charlotte. He turned on his side, staring at the crumpled hoodie on his desk chair. Her note still sat in the pocket of his sketchbook, pressed between pages like a fossil.

She liked him. She said so. And more than that, she chose to write it down. Not just pretend it never happened. Not just vanish into the crowd and laugh along with Amanda. She stepped out of the cafeteria and into something messy. Complicated. That had to count for something... didn't it? He hoped that it did.

But then Rachelle's words echoed in his head again. "This isn't a game, Alex." He closed his eyes. Tomorrow morning, they'd all be there. Or they wouldn't. Either way, things wouldn't be the same anymore.

Alex reached over and clicked off the lamp. The shadows filled the room quickly. But instead of fear or unease, he felt something else. Something alive. A pull in his chest. Like gravity was shifting. Like the world had finally started to notice he existed, and it had something to show him.

5

STRONG ILLUSIONS

Alex and Rachelle were the first of the group to reach the school gates. A cold breeze slipped past them, carrying the smell of damp grass and pavement. The streetlamps cast long shadows across the sidewalk as they waited, leaning on the metal bars like sentries guarding a secret.

"You think they'll show?" Alex asked, not quite masking the hope in his voice.

"They'd better," Rachelle said. "I'm excited to practice, but will be annoyed if they chicken out."

A moment later, they heard footsteps. Hudson rounded the corner, hoodie up, a granola bar half-eaten in one hand.

"Morning weirdos," he mumbled. "Didn't sleep. I

had a dream that I melted into a puddle of goo. I thought it was a sign."

"What kind of sign is that?" Rachelle asked.

"No clue," Hudson said with a shrug. "But I came anyway."

Then Lucas arrived, headphones still around his neck, rubbing sleep out of his eyes.

"If I'm not psychic by this, I'm walking out of there, and I'm going to demand a full refund of sleep," he said.

"No refunds," Rachelle smirked. "Only secrets."

They slipped into the building like shadows, moving quickly through the maze of empty hallways. As they neared the Annex doors, Hudson slowed, frowning at the heavy silence.

Lucas stopped altogether. "So this is it, huh? Creepy hallway, chained-up doors, ominous energy? Yeah, what could go wrong? "

"Are you coming or not?" Alex asked, hand already on the lock. He turned the key.

The door creaked open.

Warmth poured out.

Not heat, warmth. The air wrapped around them like a breath. They stepped inside.

The Annex felt even larger with the four of them in it. Their footsteps echoed off the tall walls as they walked into the half-gym, half-stage room. The morning light hadn't reached the skylights, but something unseen lit the space in a dusky gold glow.

"Okay," Hudson said. "Now what?"

Alex turned to Rachelle. "Ready?"

She grinned. "Try not to drop me."

He raised his hands, fingers twitching.

Rachelle rose into the air.

She hovered three feet up, then five. Her legs kicked slightly for balance, but Alex steadied her with a smooth motion, moving her through the air in slow, swooping arcs. Then he spun her deliberately, gently, like a dancer.

That's when she lit up. Thin darts of flame shot from her fingers in timed bursts, each one curving and streaking through the air in a wild spiral around her. The fire didn't touch her, didn't burn anything; it moved with her. Like they were in sync. Like they belonged. It was breathtaking.

"Whoa," Hudson whispered. "Okay, that's not normal."

Alex lowered her to the ground. Her shoes hit the tile with a soft tap.

Then he turned to the others. "Want to try?"

Hudson didn't hesitate. "Yeah. Lift me."

Alex reached out, and with a grunt of effort, Hudson rose a foot off the floor.

"Whoa... whoa okay, don't spin me..."

Alex laughed and moved him in a gentle arc before lowering him.

Lucas stepped forward, cautious. "This is so weird."

"Trust me," Alex said.

He lifted Lucas too, lighter, easier. Lucas hovered, grinning nervously, then flailed a little as Alex spun him slowly once and let him down.

Hudson stepped back, breathing hard. "Okay. That was insane. But I don't think that's my thing."

He looked at the broken corner of the room, a collapsed chunk of brick wall from some renovation decades ago.

Hudson walked toward it and put his hands on the crumbled edge. Grit crumbled under his fingers. He took a deep breath, braced his legs... and lifted.

The whole broken segment, easily twice his size, came off the ground.

Hudson's muscles bulged beneath his hoodie, eyes wide. "Guys...!"

He staggered once, then set it down as if it weighed nothing.

Lucas let out a low whistle. "You just benched a building, Hud."

"I feel like I could punch through a bus," Hudson grinned. "This is insane."

Then everyone turned to Lucas.

He stood with his arms crossed, frowning.

"I'm not feeling anything," he muttered. "No floating rocks. No tingly hands. No laser eyes. I don't know, maybe I'm just boring."

"Try doing something," Rachelle said. "Focus. Think of what makes you... you."

Lucas rolled his shoulders, then closed his eyes.

Alex, Rachelle, and Hudson continued showing each other what they could do. Hudson wanted to throw something large and see if Alex could levitate it so it didn't hit the ground. Rachelle looked over at Lucas. He was sitting with his eyes closed. He was surrounded by snakes.

"Lucas... Lucas, open your eyes. Move slow," she called to him.

Alex and Hudson looked too. They saw the snakes as Lucas opened his eyes. The snakes disappeared.

"What was that?" Rachelle asked. "Are you okay?"

"What happened?" Lucas asked.

"You were surrounded by snakes." Rachelle explained.

"I saw them." Hudson added.

"I was trying to focus, but my mind wandered to a documentary about snakes that I saw last night." Lucas explained.

"Try again," Alex said.

He pictured something, and then it happened.

The far wall shimmered. A glowing portal appeared,

just for a moment, and then vanished, replaced by what looked like a full-blown treasure vault, gold coins glittering under beams of sunlight that weren't real.

Everyone gasped.

Lucas opened one eye. "Did I do something?"

"You did that," Alex said. "It looked real."

Hudson tossed a rock at the illusion. It passed through, clinking against the real wall behind it. The whole thing flickered, then dissolved into sparks.

"Holy crap," Rachelle said. "You can project stuff."

Lucas just stared at his hands. "I thought about the game I was playing last night. I wanted to see it. And it showed up."

"Your brain renders illusions," Alex said. "Like a projector."

Lucas grinned slowly. "Okay. Worth waking up for."

The five of them stood in the center of the room, silent for a moment, the air buzzing with something like electricity.

They weren't just four weird kids anymore.

They were something else.

A circle forming.

A team building.

And whatever came next, whatever this Annex had given them, it had just begun. Alex felt better now that they all shared the secret.

. . .

THEIR FIRST PERIOD WAS ELECTRIC. Alex barely heard a word Mr. Willy said about colonial tensions. None of them did. His hand twitched over his notebook as he tried not to smirk. Across the room, Lucas twisted his hand clockwise into a fist under the desk. **"You see that?"**

Hudson had a big, obvious grin as he answered with a fist tap: **"Unreal."**

Rachelle added a flicking thumb like a lighter, their new shorthand for her fire skills.

Alex responded by pointing to his temple, then extending his hand, mimicking levitation. They were practically buzzing in their chairs.

Every few minutes, Charlotte glanced over. And every time she did, the signals stopped. Like a switch.

They weren't being mean, not exactly. But a line had been drawn, and she was outside it.

She pretended not to notice. Mr. Willy handed Charlotte her notebook and simply said, "make better choices." She thought he meant something he saw in her notebook, but then she wondered if it was about more. She looked at Alex, ignoring the lecture going on in front of her.

Charlotte turned her eyes back to her notebook.

She bit the edge of her pen and stared blankly at the board. But Alex saw it.

The way her jaw tightened. The way her smile never quite reached her eyes, not like it used to.

After the end of second period bell, the four of them met briefly near the drinking fountains, their faces still flushed with excitement.

Lucas leaned in, voice low. "Okay. I have a plan."

"That's never a comforting phrase," Rachelle muttered.

"No seriously. Friday. We call in sick."

Alex blinked. "What, all of us?"

"Yeah. Just once," Lucas said. "Think about it. We're in the Annex for twenty, thirty minutes tops each day, and already we're doing wild stuff. What if we stayed all day?"

Rachelle frowned. "You want to skip school?"

"Not skip. Excuse. Like when your parents call in. Mental health day. Sore throat. Grandma's funeral. Whatever works."

Hudson looked around, eyes darting. "You think it's safe to stay there that long?"

Alex answered without hesitation. "I think it's worth finding out."

Rachelle was quiet for a moment, then nodded. "One day. We learn everything we can. Then we decide what's next."

Lucas grinned. "Perfect. Operation Annex Friday. We'll bring food. Drinks. I'll smuggle in a Bluetooth speaker."

Hudson chuckled. "I'll bring dumbbells. See if my strength works on reps."

Alex laughed, but it faded quickly.

Charlotte was coming down the hallway, books clutched to her chest, her ponytail swaying as she walked.

Their laughter stopped.

Nobody spoke.

She passed them without a word, her eyes flicking to Alex just long enough for him to see the look on her face, just long enough for it to gut him a little. It was her choice, but he still felt sorry for the way she was feeling.

She smiled at him weakly. Not because she was happy. But because she wanted to look like she was.

Then, she was gone.

Rachelle watched her leave, arms crossed. "She made her choice."

"Doesn't mean she's happy with it," Alex said quietly.

Lucas opened his mouth to say something, then stopped.

No one disagreed. Because it was true.

Charlotte had chosen the popular kids, the safety,

the structure of status — but her face said it cost her something. Most kids would have done the same.

But maybe she wasn't done choosing yet.

The four of them sat at their usual lunch spot, tucked along the edge of the cafeteria in the corner that gave them just enough privacy to feel like it was their own space. Their trays were mostly ignored, a half-eaten bag of chips sitting between them, and Hudson absently bouncing a grape off his fork.

"Okay," Lucas said, lowering his voice, "we each call in Thursday night or early Friday. Parents won't do it for us, so we do it ourselves. The excuse line doesn't check; it's all just voicemail."

"I can sound like my mom easily," Hudson said confidently. "I just need a coffee mug and a sigh."

Rachelle rolled her eyes. "I'll use my dad's cell. He never notices when it's missing."

Alex laughed, then added, "I'll call my mom from the back porch. She'll think she did it and forgot."

Lucas smirked. "Flawless criminal network."

They all leaned in closer, conspiratorial.

"No supervision, no schedule, no classes," Rachelle said. "Just us, the Annex, and whatever we can figure out before someone finally notices that room exists."

Hudson raised his juice box in a toast. "To powers."

They all bumped their drinks together, plastic tapping plastic.

Alex felt something shift. Not just the plan. Not just the excitement. He looked at Rachelle as she leaned back, laughing at something Lucas said. Her curls bounced slightly, and a dimple appeared just briefly in her cheek. Her firepower had made her seem fierce, untouchable that morning, but now, in the sunlight, with peanut butter on her tray and a smudge of ink on her thumb, she looked different.

Pretty.

Not in a flashy, polished Charlotte way.

In a way that felt real.

Alex looked at her just a second too long.

And when he blinked, he noticed Charlotte watching.

She stood across the courtyard near the vending machines, with Amanda and the usual crew, but her body was turned slightly toward their table. Her eyes were locked on Alex. Then flicked, just briefly, to Rachelle. And back again.

She didn't smile this time.

She looked... unreadable.

Then Amanda nudged her, and she turned away, putting on her practiced face, like she hadn't seen anything at all.

But Alex had.

And it stuck with him longer than he wanted it to.

The bell rang for seventh period, and Alex ducked

out of the crowded hallway with a muttered excuse to a teacher he didn't even register. He wasn't headed to class. Not yet. He needed air. Space. Thought.

The hall outside Room 117 was quiet. Most of the students had already settled in. Through the narrow window in the door, Alex spotted her.

Charlotte.

She sat near the back, arms crossed loosely over her notebook, her expression distant. She wasn't pretending to pay attention; she was staring at the window. At him.

Their eyes met.

For just a second, neither of them looked away.

Then, without a word, she stood. She grabbed the bathroom pass from the wall hook and walked out.

She didn't say anything as she passed him. She just nodded once and turned down the side hallway.

Alex hesitated only a moment, then followed.

She stopped just beyond the drinking fountain, beside the side exit that nobody ever used. The light from the narrow windows above painted soft lines across the floor. Quiet settled in between them.

Charlotte turned to face him.

"I'm not going to apologize again," she said. "I already wrote it in the note."

"I read it," Alex said. "I kept it."

She nodded slowly. "I meant it."

He waited.

She looked down at her hands. "I thought it would feel like it was before, staying with Amanda and the others. You know, choosing them. I thought it'd feel smart. Strategic."

She laughed, but it didn't reach her eyes.

"But it feels like I'm living in someone else's house. Wearing clothes that don't fit. And today at lunch when I saw you all together, laughing, planning something..."

She looked up.

"I knew I was on the wrong side of the glass. I did recognize the risk you guys took to include me. I didn't appreciate what I could have had with your group. "

Alex shifted, his backpack slumping lower on one shoulder. "We didn't mean to hurt you."

"You didn't," she said. "You're just... protecting each other. I get that."

"I believe you," he said quietly. "About the note. About not telling."

Charlotte's jaw tensed. "I wouldn't betray you. Not ever."

He nodded slowly.

For a moment, all the background noise — the distant hum of classroom voices, the soft buzz of the overhead lights — faded into something more fragile. More human.

Charlotte stepped a little closer, not enough to close the space, but enough that her voice dropped.

"You looked at Rachelle today," she said, not accusing, just observing. "Not like a friend."

Alex blinked. "You noticed that?"

"I noticed you." Her voice cracked just slightly. "Even when I wish I didn't."

She pulled her sweater sleeves over her hands and looked away. "I'm not asking you to choose. I just needed to say it. Out loud. Because I hate the way it feels when everything's left unsaid."

Alex swallowed.

"Thanks," he said. "For saying it."

Charlotte gave a small, tired smile. "See you tomorrow?"

"I hope so."

Then she turned and walked back toward her classroom.

Alex stood there a moment longer, alone in the hallway, his heart thudding against his ribs.

Nothing was simple anymore. But maybe, just maybe, that meant something real was beginning.

The final period of the day was dragging on like a bad dream in slow motion. The clock on the wall above the whiteboard ticked so loudly it felt like it was mocking him.

Alex sat halfway back in the room, his math textbook open, pencil in hand, but the numbers on the page blurred into shapes that meant absolutely nothing.

His teacher, Mr. Ervin, was talking about parabolas. Or maybe triangles. Or possibly a tragic attempt at keeping kids awake with graphs. Alex had no idea.

His mind wasn't here.

It was bouncing between two impossible things.

The Annex.

He thought of the air there, thick with warmth and mystery. The way Rachelle had spun through the air like a spark, the way the fire danced from her fingers like it had always belonged to her. Hudson casually tossed concrete like it was a pillow. Lucas created full-blown illusions, like magic flowing from his brain.

And me, Alex thought. *I can move things. Float people. Lift walls. Spin metal like it's paper.*

The excitement twisted in his chest like a coil. Tomorrow, they'd be there all day. What else could they do? What was the Annex really hiding?

But then came a second thought.

Rachelle.

Charlotte.

He sighed and rested his chin in his palm.

Charlotte had opened up to him in the hallway honestly, raw, maybe even a little heartbroken. She'd made her choice... and seemed to regret it. He hadn't expected that kind of truth from her. And he liked her.

Of course, he did. She was beautiful and sharp and mysterious in her own way.

But Rachelle...

She'd been his shadow since kindergarten. She joked with him when no one else got it. She trusted him with fire. Literally. She lit up around him, and he couldn't stop seeing her differently since the Annex changed everything.

He caught himself scribbling in his notebook.

A flame.

A floating stone.

A pair of eyes.

Two different smiles.

He crossed them out and flipped the page.

This is stupid.

But it wasn't.

Because suddenly his life was full. Of choices. Of secrets. Of danger and potential and girls who looked at him like he mattered. He glanced at the clock again. Ten minutes left. Maybe, just maybe, he'd get answers tomorrow. Or everything would fall apart. Either way... he wasn't ready to go back to normal ever again.

The group chat was buzzing that night.

Lucas:

Tomorrow will either be the greatest day of our lives or the day we die. Just saying.

Hudson: I called in already. I used my sick voice and everything. I think it would have fooled even my mom.

Rachelle:

LOL, I just used my dad's phone. He won't notice it's missing until Monday.

I'm packed and ready. Snacks. Hoodie. Flashlight. Let's go.

Alex:

Snacks?? I brought a new padlock, a flashlight, and my anxiety. Does that count?

Lucas:

GREAT. Alex is bringing vibes

Hudson:

Do we have an escape plan if, like, the school catches on fire or something?

Rachelle:

I am the fire.

Alex:

Rachelle is hot lol.

Rachelle:

I mean yeah.

Lucas:

Copy that. Operation Fake Sick is a go.

Also got the Bluetooth speaker for Vibe enhancement.

Mood music while we accidentally create a new dimension.

Hudson:

I swear, if I rip a door off the wall, I'm keeping it as a trophy.

Rachelle:

Everyone bring a notebook too. We need to start writing this stuff down.

Alex:

Agreed. New rule: we document everything.

Lucas:

Including who dies first. Hudson, probably. Sorry, bro.

Hudson:

Rude. But fair.

Alex:

See you all in the morning. Try to sleep. Big day tomorrow.

Rachelle:

Night, team.

Let's find out who we really are.

Lucas:

Cue dramatic music.

Hudson:

Cue poorly timed fart jokes.

Alex saw another text.

Charlotte:

Thinking of ya.

ALEX DIDN'T KNOW how to respond. After struggling with what to say. He simply sent.

Alex: :)

He tried to get some sleep. Tomorrow was going to be big for the group.

PROFICIENT POWER

It was hinting at dawn when Alex reached the gate. The school loomed in that weird twilight state between asleep and just starting to wake.

He waited only a minute before Rachelle showed up, hoodie pulled tight around her face and steam rising from her travel mug.

"You ready for this?" she asked.

Alex grinned. "I was born ready."

"You liar." Her eyes rolled playfully.

"Fair," he said in response to her shoulder bump.

Hudson arrived next, carrying a gym bag like he was going to practice. Hudson was more puppy-like than the rest of them. He was always loyal, even when they didn't desire it. He was the most: "just go with the flow" of everyone in the school.

This wasn't practice. This was real.

Finally, Lucas came around the corner. Lucas was completely dependable but definitely operated on his own time schedule. If you accepted his pace, you would never be let down.

Inside the school, the air was still and cold, like the building had not yet awakened. A faint hum came from somewhere deep in the walls, a tired mechanical sigh that made the silence feel alive. Overhead, the fluorescent lights flickered at half-strength, bathing the hall in a jittery, pale glow that made every corner look like it was moving just slightly.

Why does every school look like the set for an apocalyptic movie? Alex mused.

Their footsteps echoed down the corridor, sharp and out of place in the quiet of the morning. The floor beneath them was scuffed and stained with years of wear, dragged desks, muddy sneakers, and shuffling feet of the involuntary population. The walls were painted the same institutional beige, but the paint had bubbled and cracked in places, like the building was shedding its skin.

They slipped into the narrower and darker side corridor where the lights didn't quite reach. The air here was colder still, carrying the faint scent of dust, old paper, and floor wax. At the end, the chained double doors loomed, painted steel, chipped and scratched around the handles. The chain was rusted in spots, padlocked tight, like a warning instead of protection.

One of the doors bore a long dent, the kind that doesn't happen by accident. A strange warmth seemed to bleed faintly from the seam between them, just enough to make the skin on their arms prickle.

When they reached the chained doors, Alex pulled out his key, but the lock wouldn't turn. He picked the lock but wondered why his key didn't work. Did someone change the lock? Did someone know it had been tampered with? Alex dismissed the thought, for bigger things waited inside.

"Everyone in."

One by one, they filed through into the dim hallway beyond. Then Alex leaned back out, hooked the chain around the bars from the inside, and pulled it tight, reaching just far enough to click the padlock shut on the outside.

It looked exactly the way they'd left it: sealed, forgotten. But on the inside, it was wide open.

They stepped deeper into the Annex, past the dusty hallways and cracked tiles, through the quiet rustle of vents that didn't seem to work but somehow still breathed. Sunlight filtered faintly through high windows, casting beams onto long-forgotten floors.

"This place still creeps me out," Lucas whispered, setting down his bag

"I love it," Rachelle said simply.

Hudson cracked his knuckles with a sound like dry twigs snapping. "So... what now?" he asked, his voice echoing faintly off the cracked tile and rusted beams above them.

Alex turned slowly, taking in the large open room, the strange half-gym, half-theater space. "We train," he said, his voice steadier than he felt. "But first..."

He raised both arms out at his sides, fingers splayed. The room responded. Debris — broken chairs, rusted scaffolding, loose tiles, scattered bricks — rattled, then lifted into the air as if caught in a slow-motion explosion. Dust fell off as the objects rose, trembled, and floated in place. With a subtle sweep of his hands, Alex directed it all into a tidy pile at the far wall, clearing the center of the room.

"I was wondering," he said, breath tight with focus, "if I could handle moving multiple things at once. And now I am curious what my limit is."

Lucas let out a low whistle, grinning as he leaned back against a cracked pillar. "I wish you could do that to my room," he said. "Would save me at least three arguments a week with my mom."

The others exchanged impressed glances, a subtle charge passing through the group — anticipation, pride, and maybe a flicker of fear. The Annex had changed them, and now, they were about to explore just how much.

They got to work.

Alex sat and practiced fine control. He could now levitate many objects — rocks, a metal ruler, and Rachelle's thermos — each spinning in different orbits. He moved them faster, slower, and paused them midair. His fingers twitched with every motion. He held several small stones. He moved one out of his hand to hit a target across the room and then back to his hand. He nodded to Rachelle.

Rachelle upped her game too. Her flames were very precise now. She could shape a whip of fire and snap it like a real one, curl a flame into a slow-burning orb the size of a softball, and even draw fiery letters in the air that hovered for seconds before fading. She could even hold a flame just to light her way.

"Who needs a flashlight? Not this girl," she joked.

Hudson tested his strength. He found a section of collapsed wall, gripped the largest piece, and lifted it above his head as if it was made of cardboard. He set it down, then tried squats, presses, and at one point just sprinted the length of the Annex carrying an old cement bench.

"Man, I wish this worked beyond the Annex," he said.

Lucas struggled at first until he stopped trying to force it. Instead, he sat in the center of the room and closed his eyes. When he opened them, an illusion shimmered into view: an endless hallway branching off the real one. It looked so real that even Hudson swore he could feel the draft from it.

He made others too — a staircase that curved into the ceiling, a curtain of glass, a snarling wolf in the corner that disappeared when anyone blinked.

"I can't hold them long yet," Lucas muttered. "But they're getting clearer."

"He startled Rochelle with an illusion of the principal walking into the room." Her face dropped, and Lucas just laughed.

IN THEIR HISTORY CLASS, the one they were supposed to be in, the fluorescent lights above buzzed with that faint flickering sound that always made Charlotte feel like she was inside a fish tank. Mr. Willy was already scribbling across the whiteboard in his usual, lopsided handwriting: Reasons for the Louisiana Purchase.

Charlotte didn't bother opening her textbook. She couldn't stop looking at the seats around the room.

Empty.

Rachelle's.

Lucas's.

Hudson's.

Alex's.

All four of them.

Gone.

At first, she thought maybe they were just late. Maybe they'd trickle in one by one, breathless and smirking, sliding into their desks with muttered excuses.

But ten minutes passed. Then fifteen.

Still nothing.

Her pencil hovered over her notebook, unmoving.

Where are they?

She tried to shake it off. Maybe Hudson's mom had picked them all up for something. Maybe they had a school project. Maybe she didn't know. But that wasn't it. She knew it wasn't. It tugged at her that she was missing out, not even sure what she was missing.

Because at lunch yesterday, she'd seen them.

Huddled together.

Laughing. Whispering. The energy between them was sparking like a live wire.

They'd gone silent the second she passed. Charlotte had felt it like a slap, the way their eyes shifted, the way Alex looked away just a beat too quickly. Something had been happening.

Planning.

And she wasn't part of it. She told herself she didn't care. But now? Now, looking at those four empty desks, the silence where their presence usually lived, it felt like a physical ache.

Especially Alex's seat.

Right there. Middle row. Slightly crooked because the leg was loose and they never bothered to fix it.

She stared at it. And missed him.

His stupid half-smile. His nervous pencil tapping. The way he looked at people when he thought no one was watching.

Charlotte blinked fast and looked down at her notes. Or tried to. The words on the page were just lines and curves.

She didn't care about the Louisiana Purchase.

She cared about the four kids who weren't here. Who were somewhere else. Together.

Doing something without her. And the worst part was, she couldn't blame them.

She'd tried to keep her foot on both sides of the line. Half in. Half out. Wanting to belong to both worlds. Afraid to lose either. But now... now it felt like she'd already lost one. The one she realized was the one that meant something, not just the illusion of something.

Charlotte drew a tiny flame in the corner of her

notebook. Just a sketch. Just a thought. Not even sure why.

She saw a curious item on the teacher's desk. It looked like a padlock, but it was mangled and cut. It seemed out of place. Mr. Willy didn't give off a handyman vibe.

She stared back at Alex's empty seat a second longer.

Wherever you are... I wish I was with you.

"Still making poor choices?" Mr. Willy asked, looking in her direction.

She startled at the question, "What?"

"I asked about which states came about from the Louisiana Purchase?" Mr. Willy clarified.

THEY TOOK BREAKS IN BURSTS, their bodies tiring before their minds, and wandered the Annex's dusty expanse in slow, curious arcs. It was like exploring the ribs of some long-dead creature, its secrets left behind in bone and shadow. Everywhere they looked, the building offered strange, disquieting details that made them pause mid-step and glance at one another, as if to confirm they were really seeing the same thing.

In the half-theater room, the sound of their footsteps echoed off the strange ridges along the curved walls, too narrow to be shelves, too symmetrical to be a defect. Rachelle ran her fingers along one and jerked back. "They're warm," she whispered.

Lucas tilted his head, squinting up. "Are they like rails... or tracks?"

Further down the west wing, they discovered what looked like an old science lab, but it had been scorched.

Burnt tile curled up at the corners, and black marks licked across the counters like shadows left by flames. In one drawer, Rachelle found a pair of cracked goggles, lenses fogged and webbed with fractures. She held them up, and the group stared silently at the faint smear of ash along the bridge. No one said it out loud, but they all felt it: something had gone wrong here.

They passed by an elevator shaft behind a warped maintenance door. The shaft yawned open, wide and dark, but there were no buttons, no cables, no signs of mechanics. Just a metal platform hanging like an idea someone had abandoned, and a rusted lever embedded in the wall beside it. Hudson gave the lever a tug, but it broke off the wall.

"Whoops," he muttered as he tossed it onto a heap of other broken objects.

Throughout the Annex were voids that defied simple explanation, crawl spaces that bent at strange angles, vents large enough to crawl through, but that led nowhere or circled back impossibly. In a side room, they found a mural on the ceiling, a swirl of stars and animals painted in vivid brushstrokes. Foxes with too many eyes. A whale curled around the moon. Deer with golden horns leaping through constellations. The image was incomplete, with half the ceiling still raw concrete.

"It feels like…" Rachelle began, then trailed off.

"Like someone started to dream here," Alex finished, voice low, "and never woke up."

They stood quietly for a long minute, the silence of the Annex wrapping around them like fog. Every crack in the floor, every rusty hinge, every echo of their breath felt like a question left unanswered. But they kept searching, drawn forward not just by the mystery, but by the pulsing sense that whatever had been hidden here was meant for them to find.

Something was off, not because the cafeteria was any fuller — it was always chaos at this time — but because Charlotte couldn't focus. Every laugh jabbed like a pin. Every slamming tray echoed like a dropped weight in her chest. Every shout from across the room hit her ears as if it was meant just to jolt her. It wasn't louder today… but it felt louder, like her nerves had been rewired overnight, stripped bare and humming just under her skin.

She stirred her fruit cup, the plastic spoon scraping

the sides like it had a grudge. The artificial sweetness clung to the roof of her mouth in a way that made her want to spit it out. Amanda sat across from her, launching into another breathless tirade about her boyfriend's hoodie obsession, apparently a cardinal sin of fashion. Charlotte nodded once, maybe twice, not really tracking the words.

How can people talk so much and say nothing at all?

she thought, barely blinking as Amanda's voice floated on.

She looked up again. Still no sign of them.

No Alex.

No Rachelle.

No Hudson.

No Lucas.

Gone.

Not just absent.

Vanished.

It had started as a twinge in first period, just a flicker of confusion, someone missing in the usual sea of faces. But now, by lunchtime, it had grown into something colder, sharper. Dread with teeth.

She shifted in her seat, casually scanning the cafeteria again, eyes flitting past every familiar face. A blonde laughing too hard. A kid in a hoodie slumped over his tray. A couple were arguing near the vending machine. But none of them were the people she wanted to see.

Their table, their spot in the corner, against the wall with the weird, chipped paint, was empty. Not just unoccupied. Abandoned. The surface looked cleaner than usual, wiped down as if someone had erased them from it entirely.

She'd checked the hall. No backpacks stuffed in the usual hidey-spots. She'd made an excuse to swing past the library. Nada. No whispers between the stacks, no scrapes of a chair pulling back where Lucas liked to sit. The courtyard had been just as empty. Just other students, oblivious and buzzing with normalcy.

But this wasn't normal.

And it wasn't random.

They hadn't all gotten sick. Not at the same time. Not without notice. Not without a single slipped explanation or request for work. Nothing.

This was planned.

And not just any plan.

The plan.

She had seen the intensity of their discussion

yesterday. They hadn't dared to speak loudly enough. But was this the plan?

The one they'd cooked up yesterday at lunch when she walked by and the conversation died. When Alex avoided her eyes and Rachelle clamped her mouth shut like Charlotte was a threat.

She could feel her pulse climbing, her fingers digging into the edge of her lunch tray.

What were they doing?

Where were they?

Why didn't she choose to be with them?

No one around her noticed. Not Amanda. Not Marissa. Not the seventh-grade girls at the edge of the table trying to edge into the cool-girl orbit. They were talking about memes and where to hang out more over the weekend.

Charlotte couldn't care less.

Her stomach twisted.

Not with jealousy, though that was part of it, but with fear. That whatever they were doing was the beginning of something big.

And that she'd already been left behind. Correction, taken herself out.

She stood abruptly.

"I need to go to the bathroom," she mumbled.

Amanda barely looked up. "Again?"

Charlotte didn't answer. She moved quickly,

weaving through the lunchroom, her eyes darting to every doorway, every teacher, every shadow, like something might slip through it.

They were somewhere. She knew that.

And wherever they were... they were probably having a lot more fun than she was.

Charlotte bit her lip hard enough to sting.

She didn't know what was worse, being shut out... or realizing she was the one that shut herself out.

By mid-afternoon, they sat in a circle, eating from chip bags and laughing between sips of warm Gatorade.

"This place is..." Hudson started, but didn't finish. Alex nodded. "I know."

None of them needed to say it.

The Annex was changing them.

Not just their powers. Them.

By the time the sun dipped low enough to leave the Annex in long shadows, they had learned things they never expected: Alex could float himself off the ground for full seconds before dropping. Rachelle could snuff out flames just as easily as she created them. Hudson could feel when something heavy was near him, like his strength was tuning to mass. Lucas managed to create a perfect illusion of Rachelle that fooled even her for a second. They packed up in silence, the day settling into their skin like warmth after a long storm.

Before they left, Alex turned back and looked into

the dim hallway behind them. The Annex called to them. Still full of secrets. Still drawing them in. He blinked and rubbed his eyes. He saw someone; it looked like a little girl.

Naw, it had to be Lucas messing with him.

Later that evening, lying in bed, Alex stared at the notification on his phone.

Charlotte: Hey. Can we talk?

Alex had to assume something was wrong; this is not normal Charlotte banter.

Alex:

Hey. Everything okay?

Charlotte:

No. Not really.

You and your crew ghosted the entire

school today.

Alex:

...yeah.

Charlotte:

And I know I'm not "in," but I'm notdumb either.

Something's happening. And you're part of it.

And I want in.

Alex:

Charlotte…

Charlotte:

Don't "Charlotte" me like I'm fragile.

You know I'm not.

Alex:

It's not that. It's just…

You don't know what you're asking.

Charlotte:

You're right. I don't.

But I do know I've been playing in the shallow end with people who only care about selfies and gossip.

You guys? You're different.

Real.

Weird, maybe. But authentic.

I miss that. I miss being with real friends.

Alex:

You are seen.

At least... I see you.

Charlotte:

Then don't leave me behind.

Alex:

It's not safe.

Charlotte: Nothing ever is.

You think I don't feel it? Whatever's going on, it's big. And I can feel it in my bones.

I don't want to be the girl watching from across the room anymore.

Alex:

...this isn't a game.

Charlotte:

Good.

Because I'm done pretending.

Alex:

I'll talk to the others.

But no promises.

Charlotte:

Fair.

But I'm not going away.

Alex:

I didn't think you would.

You never do.

Charlotte:

Let me in, Pleeeeease

MORE GIRL SORCERY.

Alex:

Fine, be at the front gate, 6a.m.

HE DIDN'T HAVE the will to tell Charlotte no, and he definitely didn't have the heart to tell the gang, especially Rachelle. The classic ask for forgiveness, not permission.

CHOOSE AGAIN

The morning was cold when Charlotte found Alex waiting near the gate. It scraped against her cheeks and left her breath hanging like fog in the stillness. A single crow croaked from a nearby tree, then flapped away, wings slicing the air like knives.

She wasn't even sure he'd show... but there he was.

Hood up, hands stuffed deep into his jacket pockets, pacing tight circles in the frost-dusted concrete like he was trying to wear a hole in it. The weight of something unspoken clung to him, making his shoulders round forward, his breath coming a little faster than the cold required. His shoes scuffed the ground softly, rhythmically. Not nerves, something heavier. Guilt, maybe. Or fear.

Charlotte crossed the lot, her boots crunching on

stray leaves. Her heart thudded with each step, louder than it should have in the quiet.

Alex looked up before she spoke, as if he'd sensed her coming.

"You came," he said, not sounding surprised, just relieved in the way someone sounds when they let go of a fear.

"You said you'd talk to them," she replied, voice low but steady.

"I didn't."

She blinked, the cold tightening around her spine. "Wait, what?"

"I didn't tell them." He exhaled, the breath rising in a plume. "I don't think they would have understood. Not yet."

His face was pale in the dim security light, but his eyes were steady, fierce, even. He turned to face her fully, shoulders squared now, the hesitance gone.

"But I trust you," he said. "So if you want in... this is it."

A gust of wind stirred her hair across her cheek. Charlotte tucked a strand behind her ear, eyes locked on his. Her fingers itched in her gloves, not from fear, but from anticipation. The sense that everything ahead was going to change, and she had just a heartbeat left to remain who she was before it started.

She hesitated, but only for a second.

Not because she was unsure.

Because she knew.

Knew what it meant to cross a line you couldn't uncross.

Knew this wasn't about curiosity anymore; it was about belonging. About choosing to step into the unknown not as a tagalong, but as a player.

Then she nodded, jaw tight with resolve. "Let's go."

And as they turned together toward the edge of the building, toward the annex and all the strangeness wrapped inside it, Charlotte felt something strange settle in her chest. Like an old key finally clicking into place.

They slipped through the side hall, feet soft on the tile, the building still cold with sleep. Alex led without speaking, his steps practiced, like the path was already a part of him.

They reached the double doors. Still chained. Still seemingly locked from the outside.

Alex reached into his pocket, pulled out his key, and with a flick of his hand, undid the lock.

Charlotte raised an eyebrow. "No turning back now."

"Nope."

The doors groaned as he pushed them open. Warmth hit her immediately, not just in temperature, but like a hug from a loved one. The air felt charged.

Like the world on the other side of the threshold was under a different set of rules. She followed him in.

The Annex was darker than she expected. Quieter. Like a museum long after hours. The walls breathed dust and forgotten time.

"Okay..." Charlotte whispered. "What is this place?"

Alex smiled faintly. "That's the first question we all ask. No answers yet."

They passed through the boiler hall, around a collapsed staircase, and into the space that was half-gym, half-stage, all magic. The same room where everything had begun.

Alex stopped near the center and turned to her. "Are you sure you want this?"

Charlotte looked around slowly. The cracks in the ceiling. The smell of old heat and rust. The echo of something humming under the floorboards.

Then she looked at him. "I'm already in. Show me."

Alex took a slow breath, spread his fingers, and reached for the surrounding air.

The air shimmered, just slightly, and a handful of loose pebbles from a broken corner lifted into the air, spinning around them like lazy satellites.

Charlotte's mouth dropped open.

"Is this real?" she whispered.

"Yeah."

"And... this happened to you? Here?"

He nodded. "All of us. One by one."

Charlotte reached out, letting a rock graze her fingertips.

"I don't want powers," she said softly. "Not really. I mean, I'm not expecting them. I just want to be… where it matters."

"You're here," Alex said. "That matters."

Charlotte stepped closer, eyes still tracking the pebbles orbiting them.

For the first time in weeks, maybe months, she felt grounded.

And lifted.

All at once.

Charlotte stood in the center of the hollow room, her boots scuffing against the dusty concrete. She looked small there, beneath the broken rafters and half-lit ceiling, like a character in someone else's dream.

Alex rubbed his hands together, nervous energy crackling faintly between his palms like the fizz before a storm. The space around them seemed to hush in anticipation, dust hanging in the air like golden snowflakes suspended in time.

"Okay," he said, voice low but sure. "I want to try something. If you're up for it."

Charlotte raised an eyebrow, the corner of her mouth curling into a teasing grin. "That depends. Is this going to end with me upside down?"

"No," he said quickly, eyes wide. "Hopefully."

"Hopefully?"

Alex winced, rubbing the back of his neck. "I mean, no. Definitely no."

That earned him a laugh — light, crystalline, and completely real. It echoed faintly in the vastness of the Annex, as if it belonged there.

"Alright," she said, brushing a strand of hair from her face. "What should I do?"

"Nothing. Just stand still. And... trust me," he said.

Charlotte hesitated, her eyes flicking briefly to the ceiling as if checking for falling debris. Then she unfolded her arms and dropped them to her sides. Her shoulders were squared. Her breath slowed.

"I trust you," she said.

Alex closed his eyes. A subtle shift stirred the room. The air thickened, not heavy, not suffocating, but alert, like the space itself had begun to lean in. A shimmer trembled in the corners of the room, one you felt but couldn't see. The dust at his feet coiled upward in lazy spirals, as if gravity were unsure of itself.

Then Charlotte rose. Slowly, steadily, like a leaf lifted by an unseen current, her boots left the floor. Her coat flared slightly with the motion, and her breath caught in a soft gasp as she floated higher. It wasn't just weightlessness; it was elegance. Each inch of her ascent felt like poetry unfolding in real time.

"Oh, okay, this is... wow, Alex."

"You're okay," he said gently. "I've got you."

Charlotte hovered at chest height, then rose until her eyes met his, suspended in a hush. Her arms stretched out by reflex, reaching for balance, but there was nothing but air and magic holding her up. It felt like standing in a dream, like the floor had forgotten to exist.

"I feel like I'm going to fall," she whispered.

"You won't," Alex replied, his voice sure. "I won't let you."

She looked at him, really looked, and something shifted behind her eyes. The flicker of fear softened, reshaped itself into awe, and then melted into something even quieter: trust.

Her arms fell gently to her sides. She let go.

Alex turned his wrist ever so slightly, and Charlotte rotated midair, slow, graceful, like a ballerina caught in the orbit of some invisible moon. Her laugh bubbled out, breathless, stunned, delighted. The sound shimmered like wind chimes in the otherwise still room.

"This is insane," she whispered.

"I know."

The Annex almost seemed to exhale around them, as if it approved.

After a few more seconds suspended in wonder, Alex carefully guided her back down. Her boots kissed the floor with a soft thump that felt louder than it should have, like waking from a vivid dream.

Charlotte stood still. She looked down at her hands, then brushed her palms over her sleeves and her ribs, as if expecting something inside her to have shifted.

But nothing had changed. No glow. No crackling surge. No spark of new power.

She held her breath, letting it go slowly, frustrated a little.

"Nothing," she murmured.

Alex gave her a small, knowing smile. "Maybe not today."

She looked up at him, not disappointed, just quietly curious. "You think I have something?"

"I think," he said, "you don't need powers to matter here."

Charlotte's smile was small, but it lingered. And for the first time since Alex had entered into her life, she didn't feel like a spectator anymore.

She felt like part of it.

The campus was stirring by the time Alex and Charlotte rounded the corner near the vending machines, where they usually met the others. The morning sun was finally warming the breeze, and students trickled in, dragging backpacks and half-finished breakfast burritos.

Lucas and Hudson were already leaning against the

wall. Rachelle sat cross-legged on the bench, scrolling through her phone, earbuds in.

The moment she spotted them, Alex and Charlotte together, she froze.

Lucas raised an eyebrow. Hudson straightened.

Charlotte hovered just behind Alex, unsure whether to smile or bolt.

Alex cleared his throat. "We need to talk."

"What's she doing here?" Rachelle snapped.

He looked at each of them in turn. "Charlotte knows something's going on. She's not stupid. She's been watching, and... she wants in."

Lucas glanced at Charlotte, then at Rachelle. "Okay, but did we talk about that?"

"No," Rachelle snapped, standing now. "Because Alex didn't give us the chance."

Charlotte flinched, but didn't speak.

"She chose this," Alex said, quieter now. "She picked us. She's not just some popular kid trying to feel important. She wants to be part of a real friend group."

"That's not the point," Rachelle said. "We're a team. We talk about these things. You don't bring people into this without asking us first."

"She's not dangerous..."

"You didn't know that yesterday," Rachelle shot back. "And you don't really know it now."

The warning bell rang long and shrill.

They stood there in a tight circle, unspoken things buzzing in the air.

Hudson sighed. "We're gonna be late."

Rachelle's jaw was tight. "This conversation's not over."

Alex nodded. "I know."

They started toward class, spreading out as they approached the door. But inside Mr. Willy's history class, the tension followed them like a storm cloud.

Alex took his seat. Rachelle slid into hers two desks in front of him, spine straight and jaw set. Lucas slouched to the left of Alex. Hudson took the far right corner, tapping his fingers nervously.

Charlotte ended up in her usual spot, quiet, alert, watching the war behind the war. Because that's what it was.

It started small. Rachelle caught Alex's eye and signed:

"You should've asked."

Alex replied,

"I had to decide."

Lucas chimed in from behind with a lazy hand flick:

"Too risky."

Alex:

"She wants to be here."

Rachelle:

"Not enough."

Hudson added:

"We're not a club. This is real."

The motions were tight, fast, and practiced. A whole conversation unfolding between glances and gestures. Charlotte's eyes ping-ponged between them, heart thudding. She could not understand every sign, not yet, but she knew enough. She knew they were arguing. About her. And then it happened.

Alex paused… then slowly made the sign for **Annex**, two fingers crossed, then pulled apart in a sweep.

Rachelle froze.

Lucas's mouth fell open.

Hudson looked like someone had punched him.

Even Charlotte could guess that one.

Everything stopped. The air thickened.

Rachelle's response was slow, sharp, unmistakable:

"You took in her in the annex?"

Alex didn't move.

Charlotte sat perfectly still. Her cheeks burned. Her hands gripped the edge of her desk.

Mr. Willy droned on about cotton tariffs. But no one was listening. Because someone had crossed a line. And there was no going back.

The bell rang for the end of second period, and the hallway exploded with bodies and sound, backpacks swinging, sneakers squeaking, voices tumbling over one another like rushing water.

But in a quiet alcove near the east stairwell, just behind a bank of old lockers no one used anymore, five students stood close, speaking in hushed tones that didn't match the frenzy just a few feet away.

Alex leaned against the wall, arms crossed. Charlotte stood beside him, unsure of where to look.

Rachelle had her hands on her hips, jaw clenched.

Lucas and Hudson stood between them all, exchanging glances like they were waiting for someone to blink first.

"So," Rachelle said, her voice low but sharp, "we're just supposed to pretend that didn't happen?"

"No," Alex said. "I'm saying it did happen. I made the call. It's done."

"You didn't have the right to do that alone," Rachelle snapped.

Charlotte flinched, but didn't step back.

"She trusted me," Alex said. "And I trusted her."

"Trust isn't the point," Lucas said, voice quieter. "The point is balance. We were a unit. You broke that."

Hudson scratched the back of his neck. "Look... I'm not saying I'm thrilled, but... can we even undo this? I mean, she knows. She's been in there."

Charlotte finally spoke, her voice surprisingly steady. "I didn't ask for this to happen like this. I didn't plan it. But I'm not going to pretend I don't want to be part of it now."

"You don't even know what it is yet," Rachelle said, eyes narrowed.

"Do any of you fully understand what it is?" Charlotte asked. "I know you're scared that I'll ruin it. But I won't."

A tense silence settled over the group.

Lucas finally sighed. "What's the alternative? Kick her out and hope she forgets everything? Hope she doesn't tell someone just because her feelings get hurt?"

Charlotte's eyes darkened. "I wouldn't."

"We can't go backwards," Alex said, looking at Rachelle now. "So it's either we figure out how to move forward... or we fall apart."

Rachelle looked at him for a long time. Something passed between them. Frustration, maybe. Or disappointment. But underneath it, loyalty, the kind that doesn't vanish just because you're mad.

She finally turned to Charlotte. "You'd better not screw this up."

Charlotte nodded. "I won't."

"We'll see," Rachelle muttered, then shouldered her backpack. "Third period."

She disappeared into the crowd. Lucas and Hudson followed, quiet and thoughtful.

Charlotte stood next to Alex for a second longer. "That could've gone worse."

Alex gave a wry smile. "You haven't seen Rachelle actually mad."

Charlotte laughed, but there was a flutter of nerves in her chest. She was in now. There was no going back.

The lunch bell rang, and the four of them — Alex, Rachelle, Lucas, and Hudson — were already waiting at their usual table when Charlotte walked up, tray in hand, hesitant but hopeful. Rachelle moved her bag off the bench, wordlessly making space. Charlotte sat.

No one said anything for a moment. It wasn't awkward exactly, just new. Like adjusting the legs of a folding table so it didn't wobble anymore.

Alex broke the silence. "So... tomorrow. We go in together. All of us."

"Before staff," Hudson said. "Like last time."

"I can bring snacks this time," Lucas offered, grinning. "We'll call it a magical brunch."

Rachelle gave him a look but appreciated that snacks were coming.

Charlotte glanced between them. "Thanks. For letting me be part of it."

Rachelle didn't smile. But she did nod.

Alex leaned forward. "We'll meet at the gate. Six sharp. Be on time."

"Agreed," Rachelle added. "We go in together. We leave together."

Charlotte nodded, more grateful than she knew how to say. But then, the silence broke.

Walking by, Amanda rang out a little too loud. "Wow. I didn't realize The Lunchables & Loners Club was the new it crowd."

Charlotte froze.

Amanda and the others — Marissa, Tori, and two other girls Charlotte barely even liked — were all watching. Amanda's smirk was picture-perfect high school cruelty, served with fries.

Charlotte ignored her.

Amanda kept going.

"I guess ditching your friends and slumming it with the weird kids is a bold choice. But hey, whatever gets you attention, right?"

Charlotte turned her head slowly. Her voice was calm. Too calm.

"Say what you want, Amanda. But at least they're real."

Amanda blinked. "Excuse me?"

"You heard me."

Lucas let out a quiet "oooh" under his breath. Rachelle's eyes narrowed, not at Charlotte, but for her.

Amanda scoffed, flicked her hair, and leaned back like she didn't care. But the pink flush on her cheeks said otherwise.

Charlotte turned back to her tray, pulse racing, hands shaking slightly, but she didn't regret it.

Not even a little.

Rachelle leaned over. "Are you sure you're ready for this?"

Charlotte nodded. "I've already made my choice."

Alex caught her eye and gave the smallest smile.

Lucas raised his juice box like a toast. "To the weird kids."

Hudson tapped his fist on the table. "And the ones smart enough to join us."

"To the real ones." Charlotte added.

The group text had a new member that night.

Lucas:

alright weirdos

tomorrow. 6 a.m.

who's bringing the cursed toaster strudel?

Hudson:

I got protein bars.

not cursed. just dry.

Rachelle:

I'll bring caffeine. If we're unlocking powers before dawn, I need a Red Bull.

Charlotte:

I can bring muffins?

Like… normal, non-magical muffins.

Alex:

Yes, bring the muffins.

The annex demands tribute.

Lucas:

speaking of the annex

what's Charlotte's power?

Hudson:

…

Charlotte:

…

does awkward social tension count?

Alex:

she didn't show anything yet

but that doesn't mean she won't.

Rachelle:

We didn't fully figure out ours on day one either.

Powers show up when you're ready. Or when they need to.

Charlotte:

I'm good either way.

Just being there with you guys is enough.

Lucas:

awww

okay now I feel like a jerk

but also still kinda hoping your power is laser eyes

Hudson:

or shapeshifting into a wolf

we need one of those

Alex:

Don't worry, Char.

whatever's in you we'll find it together.

Rachelle:

100%

Tomorrow's going to be wild.

Don't forget snacks.

Charlotte:

Thanks, guys.

Honestly.

See you at the gate, 6 sharp.

Lucas:

don't be late

or the annex eats your muffins

Rachelle:

It's Lucas's job to be late.

Alex lay in his bed, thinking of everything that had happened, and tomorrow was going to be amazing.

ALL PRESENT AND ACCOUNTED

Alex reached the gate, breath clouding in front of him. The chill wasn't as biting as it had been a week ago, but it still clung to his hoodie like a reminder that the world was still asleep.

Rachelle was already waiting, sipping from a thermos. "I got here first. Again."

Alex gave a tired grin. "I brought donuts." He pulled out a sleeve of powdered ones.

"I forgive you," she said as she pulled a donut out of the package.

Hudson showed up next, carrying a duffel bag that clinked faintly. "I brought weights."

"You brought weights?" Rachelle asked, incredulous.

"For testing," Hudson said, with a straight face. "And because I'm tired of lifting bricks."

Charlotte arrived a minute later, bundled in a scarf and jacket, with eyes wide and alert. She was carrying a small bag of pastries in one hand and a notebook in the other.

"You ready?" Alex asked.

"I think so."

Lucas, of course, showed up last, jogging up the path, breathless and holding a half-eaten granola bar.

"Okay, okay, okay, I'm here. Nobody floats off without me."

They slipped through the service hall like ghosts, the building still dark and hollow. Alex pulled out his key; the lock turned. Alex smiled, satisfied the lock hadn't been changed again.

The Annex greeted them like it always did — warm, still, and quietly watching.

Inside the central chamber, the group wasted no time. The tension of the week dissolved into movement, laughter, and focused practice.

Alex levitated himself this time, twirling slowly in the air before lifting all five muffins Charlotte had brought and rotating them like a carousel. "Magic breakfast," he said with a grin.

Rachelle smirked, then struck with a whip of fire that danced like liquid flame through the air. She split a broom handle mid-flight, then lit the pieces aflame mid-spin. It looked like a fire dancer on stage.

Hudson dropped his duffel and pulled out a small barbell. "Watch this."

He squatted, lifted it with one arm, then set it aside and walked over to a section of collapsed brick wall. With a guttural breath, he hoisted the entire pile, holding it overhead with ease. "Better than gym class."

Lucas paced in a circle, then raised his hand. The shadows shifted, and suddenly a towering stone golem rose from the wall, stomping once before vanishing in a swirl of smoke. "Still just illusions," he muttered. "But they're getting better."

Charlotte stood off to the side, taking it all in.

"You're all insane," she whispered, breath catching. "In the best way."

"You'll get yours," Rachelle said. "It'll come."

Charlotte smiled softly, still unsure.

They started packing up just as the sun began to rise through the broken windows high above.

Alex locked eyes with Charlotte. "You're part of this, no matter what."

She nodded, tucking her notebook back into her bag. Then, with a low rumble, everything changed. A section of the ceiling gave a groan and collapsed.

The concrete above them cracked free in one giant slab, breaking into chunks the size of backpacks and larger. They fell directly toward the center of the group.

Charlotte's breath caught. Everyone froze. But she moved. She didn't think, just threw her hands up and screamed. The debris hit something in midair and bounced. Chipped cement, broken wood, and twisted metal slammed into an invisible wall that shimmered for a moment like glass dipped in gold, then fell harmlessly to the sides. The group ducked and shielded themselves, but not a single rock touched them.

When the dust settled, Charlotte was standing beneath a faint glowing dome. Her arms trembled. The air around her was still warm.

Rachelle's jaw dropped. "Was that?"

Lucas blinked. "That was her."

Alex stepped forward slowly. "Charlotte... you did that."

Charlotte looked down at her hands, then up at the invisible shell fading around her. "I didn't mean to. I just... I saw it falling, and..."

Hudson let out a low whistle. "Shield powers. That's awesome."

"You saved us," Rachelle added, with genuine awe in her voice.

Charlotte looked at them all, heart pounding, a wild grin starting to take shape. "So... I guess I'm in for real now?"

"You were in before," Alex said. "But now…"

"You're one of us," Rachelle finished, a small smile breaking through.

The five of them stood in the Annex, a little dusty, a little shaken, but more together than ever.

They walked back through the dim corridors of the Annex, buzzing with adrenaline, laughter echoing softly off the old stone walls. Charlotte had saved them. With power. Real, actual, incredible power.

Rachelle kept sneaking glances at her, like she couldn't quite believe what she'd seen. Hudson was already trying to name her ability. "Forcefield Queen" didn't stick. Lucas trailed behind, unusually quiet.

As they passed under the broken archway near the boiler room, Lucas slowed. Something prickled at the back of his neck. A sudden awareness. He turned his head just slightly, just enough to catch the corner of his eye.

There.

Movement.

A dark figure, shadowed, stood just at the edge of the far corridor. Watching.

Lucas blinked, turning fast toward it. Nothing. The hallway was empty. Just dust, flickering light, and the low hum of old pipes. He squinted. Waited. Still nothing.

"Hey, you good?" Alex called over his shoulder.

Lucas hesitated, then shook his head. "Yeah. Just... thought I saw someone or something. False alarm."

Rachelle rolled her eyes. "Someone else in here? At six-thirty in the morning?"

Lucas offered a shrug, forcing a laugh. "Guess I'm still half-asleep."

But as he turned to follow the others out, he glanced back one last time. Still nothing. But the chill that slipped down his spine didn't fade.

Rachelle's curls bounced with every step. Hudson couldn't stop flexing like he wasn't even aware of it. Lucas kept making shadow-illusions of the ceiling collapsing and Charlotte saving them with a shimmering shield. Each time, it got more dramatic.

Alex just smiled, walking right in the center of them all, his hoodie dusted with dirt and glory.

They were halfway across the quad, heading back toward the real world, when they saw them.

Amanda. Marissa. Tori. And two other girls with perfect ponytails and matching sneers.

They were standing by the drinking fountain. The second they saw Charlotte with the group, they stopped talking. All five stared as they passed.

Amanda tilted her head just slightly, expression cool and calculating. Her gaze flicked to Charlotte, then to Rachelle, then back to Charlotte.

Charlotte didn't flinch.

She leaned closer to Alex, eyes still forward, voice low but proud. "They have no idea."

Rachelle smirked.

Charlotte added, just loud enough for her old friends to maybe hear: "We're tight. Tighter than they've ever been. And we have a secret."

Alex grinned. "A big one."

They walked on, Amanda's stare burning behind them like a flashlight beam that had lost its power.

By the time they hit Mr. Willy's first-period history class, any hope of focusing on the War of 1812 was laughable.

They took their usual seats like nothing was different, except everything was.

Mr. Willy turned to the board and started writing "Battle of Lake Erie", but the real battle was happening in silence, beneath desks, and in glances passed around the room.

Alex:

(Both hands in front, palms forward) **"Charlotte's shield."**

Lucas:

(Opens fist quickly) **"Epic."**

Charlotte:

(Fist rotates back and forth.) **"Still shaking."**

Hudson:

(Thumbs up, fist pump) **"You crushed it."**

Rachelle:

(Thumbs up, fist pump, taps shoulder makes fist) **"Glad, you crushed it."**

Lucas:

(Fingers making walking motion, then hands forming goggles) **"Need to explore deeper. Find more."**

Rachelle:

(One hand over heart, then tapping forehead) **"We need a plan."**

Alex:

(Finger draws a circle, taps wrist.) **"Another full-day trip. Soon."**

Charlotte:

(Touches chest, nods) **"I'm in. All in."**

THEIR FINGERS DANCED, brief taps, secret signs, like a language built from play but perfected in shared danger. Their eyes sparkled, flicking from one to another with the kind of knowing that couldn't be taught. Even though they sat beneath fluorescent lights and cracked ceiling tiles, their hearts beat as if they were still down there, in that hushed, humming, sacred place, where the world had tilted just slightly and everything impossible had started to feel real.

Each silent message passed between them strengthened their bond. The kind of bond you don't see so much as feel, knowing your back is covered.

Even Mr. Willy's monotone couldn't dull it, though he certainly tried, droning on about treaties and tariff systems as if the very fabric of their lives hadn't been rewoven hours ago.

Rachelle sat towards the front, the lighting catching in her curls like threads of copper. She glanced at the map of colonial territories tacked to the classroom wall, but her mind was somewhere else entirely. Her gaze drifted to the group. Alex, focused but twitching with restlessness; Lucas, doodling nonsense quotations into his notes; Hudson, twirling a pen between his fingers like it was a weapon; Charlotte, posture straight, but feet tapping a slow rhythm beneath her chair.

Rachelle smiled, just slightly, the corners of her mouth tugging upward with quiet certainty.

They weren't just students anymore. They were explorers of the unspoken. Survivors of the uncanny. Chosen in a way others couldn't see and definitely wouldn't understand. Something about that realization made the room seem smaller, like the walls were no longer big enough to contain who they were.

Her thoughts flickered—back to the Annex. The echoing corridors, the warm hush of the air that seemed to know them, the surreal shimmer that clung to the shadows. She could almost smell it: that old stone-and-spark scent, like rain on hot metal. Her chest tightened with the need to return.

They had been changed. Marked—not with scars or sigils, but with awareness. They knew what others didn't. They felt what others couldn't.

Rachelle shifted in her seat and made a circle with her index finger and thumb and made a circle in the air, **"safe, together"**. Behind her, Alex returned the gesture without missing a beat.

She didn't need to say anything else.

Because tomorrow, or next week, or whenever the doors would creak open again and let them slip back into that strange in-between world...

They'd go.

Together.

The lunch table was abuzz with leftover energy from the morning's adventure. Crushed chip bags, a half-eaten sandwich, and a chocolate milk sat forgotten between them as the five leaned in, voices low.

Alex was the first to say it.

"We need more time in the Annex. Like... real time. Not just forty minutes before school."

Rachelle raised a brow. "Another full-day skip? They're gonna catch on if we pull that again too soon."

"Exactly," Alex said, lowering his voice. "That's why I'm saying... Saturday."

Hudson blinked. "Wait. You're talking about breaking in on the weekend?"

Lucas perked up. "I mean... technically we already broke in. What's one more felony?"

Charlotte frowned. "How would that even work? The school's locked tight on weekends. Doors, alarms..."

Alex grinned. "Not the Annex."

Everyone looked at him.

"We switch the lock on the outer chain at the side entrance to the service corridor? We put that there. There's no alarm. The rest of the school stays locked, but the Annex entrance? If we come through the side entrance to the service corridor, we're good."

Rachelle crossed her arms, considering. "No janitors?"

"Not on Saturdays," Hudson said. "Only on Friday nights. My mom works for the district. I overheard her once."

Lucas leaned in, excited now. "So we slip in early, same time as usual. Stay as long as we want. Train, explore, maybe figure out if there's more to the place."

Charlotte added, "And no teachers wondering why we're all 'sick' again."

It grew quiet for a beat as they all let the idea settle. Sneaking in on a weekend wasn't a joke. It was bold. It was serious.

It was awesome.

"I'm in," Alex said.

"I'm in," Rachelle followed.

Hudson shrugged. "Ride or die."

Lucas gave a two-finger salute. "You know I'm down."

Everyone looked at Charlotte.

She smiled, calm but confident. "Let's do it."

Alex leaned back, grinning at the ceiling like he couldn't believe this was real. "Saturday it is."

They clinked juice boxes.

Later, Alex lay in bed, the room dark except for the faint blue glow of his phone. He scrolled for a minute, then saw Charlotte's name light up.

Charlotte 9:57 PM

hey… you up?

Alex 9:58 PM

yeah. can't sleep. too much magic in the bloodstream lol

Charlotte 9:59 PM

same. I've never felt this kind of energy before. like… I finally belong somewhere.

Alex 10:00 PM

you do. we're glad you're in it with us.

I am.

Charlotte 10:01 PM

thanks for bringing me in. I was scared I'd never be more than what Amanda and them thought of me.

Alex 10:01 PM

they never saw you.

we do.

Charlotte 10:03 PM

this group, it matters.

you matter.

and I really like being around you, Alex.

Alex stared at the screen for a long second, his heart kicking up.

Alex 10:03 PM

I like being around you too

a lot

Charlotte 10:05 PM

okay good.

gnite magic boy

Alex 10:05 PM

gnite shield girl

He set his phone down, smiling in the dark, heart still warm from the conversation. Just as he was about to close his eyes, the phone buzzed once more.

Rachelle 10:11 PM

today was amazing

have a good night ;)

ALEX STARED at the message for a long time, then liked the comment. Then he put the phone on his nightstand, lay back, and let the swirl of thoughts carry him to sleep.

Ash fell like gray snow, blanketing the fields. The farmhouse was gone, with only blackened beams jutting like broken bones against a smoldering horizon. The stench of smoke clung to the air, sour and sharp, heavy enough to choke.

Alex stood in the ruin, though in the dream he wasn't himself; he was smaller, weaker. He crouched in the tall grass, unseen, heart hammering, forced to watch.

A girl stumbled through the field. Barefoot. Thin as a reed. Her hair clung in damp ropes to her face; her cheeks were blotched with tears. Molga. Alone. Her family had gone to the place people go when they leave this world.

She clutched herself as if she could keep from coming apart. The field stretched endlessly, all shadow and silence, except for the stone well that should not have been there.

It rose from the ground as if it had always waited: old granite blocks slick with moss, the stones breathing a cold mist.

Molga's lips trembled. Her small hand dug into her pocket and pulled free a single coin, worn smooth. She held it over the mouth of the well.

"I wish," she whispered, voice raw with grief. "I wish I could be with them again… or survive, even if I'm alone."

The coin fell. There was no splash. Only silence. And then… breath.

Cold, damp, drawn up from the depths, sweeping across the field in a single exhale that stole the warmth from the night. Alex's teeth chattered. Frost webbed the grass.

And then the voice. Not loud, but everywhere. Slipping through the air, curling into the bones. "Such tender sorrow," it purred. "Such hunger to endure."

Molga flinched, but did not run. Her gaze fixed on the dark mouth of the well. "Who... who are you?"

"I am Wylithar," the voice answered, deep and silken, smooth as rot under velvet. "Dreams hurt, little one. But even in hurt, dreams can be made true, if you anchor them."

Alex wanted to scream for her to stop, to run, but his throat was sealed. His limbs refused him. He was only a shadow, a witness.

"How?" Molga whispered.

The well breathed again, and instructions poured like poison into her ear.

"Find a piece of leather. Carve your name, your full name, into it, and under the moon, speak it aloud three times. Seal it in a jar and place it here, at the mouth of the well."

Moonlight spilled suddenly over the field, pale and merciless.

Alex watched as her small hands sawed a strip from her father's worn belt. She carved clumsy letters with a knife too big for her grip. Blood welled where the blade slipped, smearing the name in crimson.

Her voice rose, shaking, desperate. Once. Twice. Thrice. She pressed the leather into a jar, placed it at the stones. The earth shuddered.

From the well, smoke bled upward, thick and writhing, until it coiled into a towering shape. Two violet eyes burned within the shadow, and the name it had been given slid from its tongue like a chain clicking shut.

"Molga."

She staggered back, eyes wide with fear and wonder.

"You have bound yourself," Wylithar the boundless intoned, voice rippling through the night. "To the ley. To the gate. You have opened the path for me, and it is your prison now. The power will keep you alive, yes. But life is a chain. And now you wear it."

The demon shook, and his form dissolved into ash, leaving the form of an ordinary man in his place. I'm going to town he said with a wicked grin. As he strode off the field fell still, but the thrum of power echoed in the earth, a heartbeat that wasn't hers.

Alex gasped, finally able to move, his chest seizing with panic. He wiped at the tears on his cheek. I gasped for a deep breath, and then his eyes opened. He was soaked in sweat, clutching his sheets. The stink of smoke was still in his nose. The tremor of that name was still beating in his ears.

Wylithar the Boundless, and the certainty that Molga had set him free.

9

PAY THE TOLL

One by one, they pulled off their carefully rehearsed escape plans.

Alex told his mom he was volunteering for a service project with Lucas. "We're helping clear out an old storage site behind the school. Some community thing." She smiled, proud. He left out the part about supernatural fire and levitation.

Rachelle claimed she was spending the day helping her aunt reorganize her vintage store downtown. Her mom believed it because Rachelle had actually done it once, and hated every second of it.

Hudson faked a mandatory robotics practice. He even got his older brother to back him up. "You know how competitive the league is," his brother said dramatically over cereal.

Lucas just said he was sleeping over at Alex's. No one questioned it. He was the king of convenient half-truths.

Charlotte said she was going shopping with her mom's cousin, who lived "like, way on the east side," so she might not have cell service all day. She set her phone to Do Not Disturb and left it in her backpack along with her conscience.

They met before sunrise at the edge of the school's perimeter fence. The sky was a hazy violet, clouds edged with gold.

Alex was first, tossing his backpack over the fence before climbing with practiced ease. One by one, the others followed, their hands scraped and knees dusty, hearts racing like fugitives.

They slipped along the side of the building until they reached the service corridor. Alex picked the lock on the door. Now inside it was a turn and then the chained doors of the Annex.

The padlock still hung there, exactly where Alex had left it.

"I can't believe we're doing this," Charlotte whispered, breath fogging.

Alex smiled. "I can."

They pushed through the doors into the warmth and hush of the Annex.

They reached the large chamber where they had

first tested their powers together. The air felt thicker here, heavier with memory. The cracked tile and shadowy corners should have made the space feel cold and industrial, but instead, it felt almost... sacred. Like the hush in an old cathedral. The soft echoes of their footsteps seemed to acknowledge their return.

The ceiling arched high above them, half-open to the bones of the building. Faded paint flaked from the support beams, and specks of dust spiraled lazily in angled rays of light that pierced through broken vents above. There was a hum here, just beneath hearing. A subtle vibration buzzed against their teeth, as if the room itself remembered.

They wasted no time.

Alex rose into the air with a slow exhale, his arms drifting outward like wings. The surrounding air shimmered faintly, warm and charged. He floated, smooth and graceful, spinning once midair just for the joy of it.

Rachelle danced fire through her fingers, glowing strands of orange and gold that curled and twirled like ribbon caught in a breeze. She laughed as the heat tickled her arms but never burned. Her eyes gleamed with wild freedom.

Hudson let out a wordless whoop and launched half a rusted vending machine across the chamber. It crashed with a metallic scream against the far wall, shaking dust loose from the rafters. "Oh man," he grinned, flexing. "That never gets old."

Lucas swept his hands in wide arcs, painting glowing creatures into the air, first a fox, then a hawk, then a dragon the size of a car, all shimmering with refracted color like sunlight on oil. They coiled and danced, casting living shadows on the cracked walls.

Charlotte stood still at first, arms raised hesitantly. A golden shimmer bloomed between her palms, thin and pulsing, flickering like candlelight in the wind. But it held. It grew. She gasped softly as the light formed a translucent shield across part of the wall, brighter and more solid with each attempt.

"I wonder how big a shield I can make?" she asked aloud.

Their voices filled the space — shouts, laughter, encouragement. They chased each other through light and power, their joy echoing in the chamber like music. This was theirs. This was where they became more than just kids hiding secrets.

They felt alive.

Until the room turned cold.

Not gradually.

It was as if something exhaled all at once, long and deep, and stole the warmth from the very air.

Instantly, the temperature dropped. Breath turned visible. Skin puckered with goosebumps.

The lights — what few still worked — flickered. Once. Then again. Then dimmed to a dull orange glow like dying embers.

Alex fell. He dropped from midair with a grunt, landing hard on one knee. "Ow, what the...?"

Rachelle's fire blinked out in a single puff of smoke. Her eyes went wide and confused, her fingers twitching with disbelief. "That wasn't me..."

Lucas staggered. His illusions shattered like soap bubbles, the colors retreating into nothing. He blinked rapidly and gasped, "They're gone. I can't..."

Hudson bent to lift a thick plank of wood, something he could've tossed like a baseball just seconds ago, but it didn't budge. He growled and tried again, straining. "No way. What the hell is this?"

Charlotte thrust out her hands instinctively. "Shield!" she whispered. Nothing. Not even a flicker. "Come on... come on!" Her voice cracked with frustration. "It's gone!"

They looked at one another, hearts hammering, suddenly aware of just how quiet the chamber had become.

No hum.

No echo.

Even their breathing sounded loud.

Then they heard it.

A voice.

Not loud, but it didn't have to be. It slipped through the air like smoke, smooth and cold, curling between their ribs and up their spines.

"You've borrowed what isn't yours."

It was a woman's voice, low, deliberate, and oddly calm. Like someone who didn't need to shout to be feared. Like someone who had been here before.

The shadows deepened.

The air thickened.

Alex stood slowly, eyes sweeping the dark edges of the room.

"Who's there?" he demanded, though his voice trembled.

Silence.

Then, soft footsteps, measured, precise.

And the feeling that the Annex was no longer theirs.

Not entirely.

Not anymore.

They turned, every head snapping toward the far end of the chamber.

A girl stood in the shadows. Pale as ash, her hair long and tangled like roots. She wore a dark cloak woven from something that shimmered like smoke. Her eyes gleamed violet in the dim light.

"This place," she said, "was mine long before your school poisoned the earth around it."

The air tightened.

"I am bound here," the girl said, stepping just into the edge of the light. Her voice was smooth as velvet but threaded with something brittle underneath. "By cold blood and old magic. This place — your precious little playground — is not a gift. It's a well. And now, because of your games, you've drawn deeply."

Alex moved forward, swallowing hard. "We didn't mean to…"

"But you did," she cut in gently, like a teacher correcting a bright but careless student. She smiled but her eyes remained cold. "Intent is meaningless to the well. Magic answers to action. And now, as with all things taken… a balance must be restored."

A hush fell over them, thick, suffocating. Even the dust in the air seemed to pause.

Rachelle's voice cracked as she asked, "What… kind of balance?"

The woman tilted her head, and for a moment she looked almost amused, almost kind. "Oh, nothing dramatic, darling. A token. A gesture. Nothing that will hurt, if given freely."

They waited.

She let the pause stretch, just long enough for discomfort to bloom.

"A lock of hair," she said at last. "From each of you.

Willingly. A symbolic tether. It seals the pact. Without it..." She glanced around at their wide, nervous eyes. "Well. You've felt it already, haven't you? The silence in your veins. Your powers, gone."

Lucas took a step back. "That's... that's witchcraft."

She chuckled low, elegant, patronizing. "Words are funny things. You call it witchcraft. I call it acknowledgement. The magic already lives within you. This only... affirms it."

Hudson squinted at her. "Why hair?"

"A lock is part of the self," she said smoothly. "Given freely, it speaks of trust. It binds nothing but intention. And trust me, your intention matters here."

Her eyes glinted like polished onyx.

They hesitated.

Charlotte looked at Alex.

He didn't nod right away. He looked at the woman, then at the dark jar she pulled from within her robes. It shimmered, glass or maybe stone, inscribed with runes that twisted like oil on water.

Finally, he nodded once, sharply, reluctantly.

The woman offered the blade. Black, small, and curved like a crescent moon.

Alex stepped forward first. She smiled warmly, too warmly, and whispered something in a language older than the walls as his lock dropped into the jar.

Rachelle followed, her fingers trembling as she cut her hair. The whisper came again.

Hudson muttered something under his breath and did it without ceremony.

Lucas cursed subtly as he offered his. "I still don't like this," he muttered.

"You will," she murmured, "when you feel whole again."

Charlotte was last.

The woman's eyes lingered on her longer than the others.

"You're curious," she said softly. "Not just about power. About purpose. About why the Annex called to you."

Charlotte didn't answer. But she cut the lock, and let it fall.

When the final piece landed, the jar pulsed once, then shimmered. The air shifted.

Warmth rushed back like a flood. The lights buzzed and came alive overhead. The weight in the air lifted. Alex inhaled sharply. The buzz of power was back in his chest, a familiar thrum.

Rachelle's fingers sparked like flint striking tinder. "Oh, yes!"

Lucas gave a short laugh. "It's back. I can feel it."

The woman turned as if the matter were settled. Her

voice trailed behind her like the hem of a dress. "You've chosen well. For now."

And just like that, she was leaving, vanishing into the dark edges of the room.

Had she always been there?

The jar remained. Sitting in the center of the room.

Still faintly pulsing.

"What did we agree to?" Rachelle called.

The woman paused. Slowly, she looked over her shoulder.

"You've traded life... for magic."

Charlotte blinked. "Wait, what?"

"You now feed the owner of this gateway," she said. "Small at first. But it adds up."

Then she vanished into smoke, like a candle blown out.

They stood there, cold again. Quiet.

Alex looked at his hand. It still hummed with power.

But now, it felt... heavier.

The silence between them said it all.

Molga knelt at the edge of the gateway, trembling. Her hands, twisted and weathered by centuries, clutched at her shawl like it could hold her together. Her chest heaved. Every breath felt heavier than the last.

She had done it. Begging the universe to forgive her, she had done it.

Those kids, those poor kids.

Five names. Five young faces, still vivid in her mind. The hope in their eyes. The trust they'd given her. He had drawn them here, step by step, the way a shepherd guides lambs into the pen. Only this pen was stone, and its gate opened onto Hell. But she was the one who had made the pact.

A cold wind rippled through the chamber. The candles bent low, nearly snuffed.

And then he was there.

Wylithar the Boundless stepped from the shadows, smoke peeling off his form as he unfolded from the darkness. His eyes glowed violet, burning through the dimness, and his voice curled through the air like chains dragged across stone; his wings hung like a leathery cape.

"My faithful child." His smile split too wide, too knowing. "I taste the bindings. I taste their fear. You have delivered your replacements."

Molga's head bowed. Her voice broke on the words. "I did... as you asked. I led them here. Five of them. Five strong, bright souls. You said..." She raised her face, streaked with tears. "You said that would be enough. That I would be free."

For a moment, silence.

Then, a low chuckle that swelled into laughter, shaking the walls.

"Free?" Wylithar stepped closer, talons scraping sparks from the stone as he walked. "Yes, yes. That was the promise. But child..." His tone coiled, amused, cruel. "The promise is not yet sealed."

Her stomach dropped. "What?"

"The pact binds at the fullness of the moon," he said, savoring each word. "Not before. Until the next moon rises in its silver crown, you are still mine. The ley is still yours to bear."

Molga's breath shuddered out. She swayed, the weight of her sin dragging her down. Her knees buckled, and she collapsed onto the cold stone. Her hands scraped at the floor as if she could claw her guilt from the earth itself.

"I damned them," she whispered, choking on the words. "I damned them all."

Wylithar bent low, his shadow falling across her broken form. His laughter rolled out again, deeper this time, rattling the chamber like thunder in a crypt.

"Guilt suits you, Molga. Wear it well. It makes the taste all the sweeter."

He straightened, striding toward the chamber's exit. With every step, his form shifted, smoke hardening into flesh, violet fire dimming to a cruel gleam in human eyes. By the time he reached the threshold, Wylithar was a man, ordinary, plain, perfect for hiding among the mortals.

His footsteps echoed as he left, laughter trailing behind him like smoke.

Molga lay in the dark, alone, the ley's pulse thrumming beneath her like a heartbeat she could never escape.

They climbed the fence one at a time, slower than usual. No one was laughing. No one was teasing.

The morning sun had fully broken over the rooftops now, turning the neighborhood gold. Cars passed on the distant street. Somewhere, a dog barked. The world kept turning, but they'd crossed a threshold and could not go back.

They started walking home together, backpacks slung heavy and hearts even heavier.

Alex was the first to speak. "We can't just... accept this."

"Agreed," Lucas said. "The whole 'you traded your life for magic' thing doesn't work for me."

"We didn't even know we were making a deal," Rachelle said, kicking at a pinecone. "We should've asked more questions."

Charlotte looked down at her hands, still aching slightly from her shield. "I just want to know what she is. A ghost? A demon? A witch?"

"She said she was bound there," Hudson said. "That

the Annex was hers. What if it's more than just the school? What if it was always a magical place?"

"I don't think it's just her, either," Alex said. "That place feels... alive. It's like it let us in."

Lucas squinted at him. "So you're saying the building itself is magic?"

"I'm saying," Alex replied, "we don't know anything, and that needs to change."

They turned onto the sidewalk near Hudson's house, slowing their pace like none of them wanted to be the first to split off.

"We need to find out everything," Charlotte said. "About the land, the history, magical contracts, whatever this is. Who else has been affected? What kind of creature she is. How to reverse a curse."

"Can we even do that?" Rachelle asked.

Lucas shrugged. "Only one way to find out. Libraries, the internet, weird old bookstores — we hit them all."

Hudson gave a tired smile. "Time to turn into paranormal nerds."

Charlotte reached into her backpack, pulled out a little notebook, and flipped to a blank page. "Okay. Step one: Research."

Alex nodded, the tension in his chest finally shifting into resolve. "Step two: Learn how to protect ourselves."

"Step three," Rachelle added, "figure out if we can beat her at her own game."

They passed the last intersection before splitting in different directions. For a moment they all stood there on the sidewalk, a quiet team bound by something deeper than friendship.

"You think we're cursed?" Hudson asked.

Charlotte looked at him, eyes steady. "I think we're in a story that hasn't finished writing itself yet."

And then they went their separate ways, books to find, searches to start, and a fire in their chests that not even magic could put out.

Lucas sat hunched at his desk, the blue light from his monitor casting long shadows across his room. Tabs were stacked in his browser like a digital sandwich — local land records, obscure blog posts, old maps, and even a ghost-hunting forum out of Phoenix.

He clicked through each, scribbling notes on a crumpled fast-food napkin.

The most promising details came from a community archive site:

The land that is now Roosevelt Junior High was once part of the Kaweah Plains. Before it was bought by the school district in the 1940s, it belonged to a defunct spiritualist commune called The Thirteen Stars. No one knows exactly what they believed, but stories mention ritual circles, "energy wells," and a guardian spirit they called the "Well Mother."

Lucas leaned back, heart thudding.

Hudson, meanwhile, had gone with the low-tech approach, Grandma.

He helped her fold laundry and asked the questions sideways, like he was writing a story. "If someone accidentally made a magical deal, like... with a spirit, how would they undo it?"

His grandma gave him a look. But instead of laughing it off, she set down a towel and thought.

"A real spirit won't always bargain fair. If someone made a deal and didn't know the terms, that's bad business. There's always a cost. But sometimes, there's a reversal too. If you can find the spirit's name, or the original place of power... sometimes you can cut the cord."

He didn't press further. But he left with a strange chill in his bones.

Alex and Rachelle met at the city library. They split up the stacks. Rachelle dove into local history while Alex explored folklore and mythology.

She found an old pamphlet scanned into a digital archive: "The Kaweah Circle: Local Spiritualist Activity in the Early 20th Century."

It mentioned unusual symbols carved into trees, a

network of tunnels near the Mountains, and a "sealed place" used for spiritual channeling.

Alex found a dusty old book on folk magic with a section titled "Bindings and Barters."

"A soul-bound spirit may trade power for time, energy, or devotion. These agreements, when made on land of magical significance, are hard to break. However, by tracing the line of the spirit's original tether, one may find a way to sever it, though not without risk."

They looked at each other, unsettled.

Charlotte, determined to contribute, took a bus to a metaphysical shop with crystal chimes and sandalwood smoke thick in the air.

The owner, a thin man in layers of linen and too many necklaces, listened carefully as she described the situation in vague terms.

"This spirit is anchored. Old. Territorial," he said. "You're in over your heads, but maybe not helpless. If she's bound to a place, there may be a way to weaken her, undo her knot. But I can't help you more than that."

He handed her a card.

"Try Tea & Truth. Across town. Old place. An older woman runs it. She knows things."

Charlotte slipped the card into her pocket, thanked him, and left more curious than ever.

They all met at Lucas's house and crammed into the

gameroom behind the garage. A worn sectional, a mini fridge, and a giant TV covered half the wall. Controllers were scattered like confetti.

"Alright," Lucas said, closing the blinds. "Everyone get in. Hudson, shut the door."

Just as they settled, the door flew open again.

"Hey losers," Trevor, Lucas's eleven-year-old brother, announced, stepping in with a mouthful of crackers. "You hiding a secret club or just being awkward together?"

"Out," Lucas said.

Trevor ignored him and flopped onto the armrest beside Charlotte.

Hudson tossed him a foam football. "Go long."

"Seriously?"

"Yup. Front yard."

Trevor shrugged and walked off, chewing loudly. "Whatever. Just don't blow up the house, nerds."

Lucas locked the door behind him.

They all sighed in unison.

"Okay," Alex said. "Let's compare notes."

They each took turns laying out what they'd found: the land's haunted past, the strange commune, the guardian spirit, the binding rules, and the cryptic hints about breaking magical contracts.

"We need to find the spirit's name," Charlotte said. "The metaphysical guy said names hold power."

"And the place she's bound," Hudson added. "There might be something deeper in the Annex, like a core."

Lucas held up his crumpled napkin, finger pointing to the words "Well Mother".

"That could be it," he said. "What the old commune called her."

"That seems more a title than a name, but we could use it to learn more," Charlotte noted.

Rachelle leaned forward. "So what's our next step? Find the name, the anchor point, the tether, whatever it is, and cut the cord?"

"Maybe," Alex said, "but if we're going to do that, we need to be smart. Be careful. She's not just some ghost. She watched us. She manipulated us."

"And she still has our hair," Charlotte added quietly.

They looked at one another, the air growing heavier with realization.

They had answers now.

But the real questions were just beginning.

The bus rumbled along the uneven road, its brakes screeching at every stop. The windows were fogged from the air conditioning, and the five of them sat huddled in the back row like a conspiracy in motion.

Lucas tapped frantically on his phone. "Okay, listen to this. There's folklore about witches being bound to land, like actually leashed to it. Either of their own doing, or because someone sealed them there."

"You mean like the spirit at school?" Hudson asked, leaning over his shoulder.

"Exactly. There's stuff about geas, like a magical contract. You get power, but it comes at a major price."

Rachelle frowned. "What kind of price?"

"Time, freedom, love... even memory. Some witches wanted to live forever, so they traded their soul, or bound themselves to a place with power, like a crossroads or crypt or cursed well."

Charlotte sat with her knees pulled up onto the seat, arms crossed. "What if she didn't want to stay? What if she had to? Like someone else did this to her?"

Alex nodded slowly. "Could explain why she's so bitter. Why she wants to feed off us. Maybe she's stuck until she finishes something... or until we finish it for her."

Rachelle muttered, "Or maybe she just wants to take everything from us."

Charlotte looked down. "Still. I felt her. She didn't seem like a monster. Not completely."

Lucas shrugged. "Monsters usually don't start out that way."

The bus groaned to a stop.

"This is it," Charlotte said.

They stepped onto the sun-bleached street, heat shimmering off the sidewalk. The Tea & Truth shop was tucked between a dusty old barbershop and a weather-beaten hardware store. Its sign, a chipped wooden board painted with curling ivy, swayed on rusted chains, creaking softly as a breeze stirred the air like an exhale.

Inside, the air changed. Warmer. Denser. It felt like stepping into a memory.

Shelves climbed the walls, cluttered with beeswax candles, tiny glass bottles crammed with herbs, crystals that shimmered without movement, and handwritten cards labeled with names like shadow veil, spirit door, and forget-me-not. The scent of dried flowers, ancient wood, and something earthy, like loam and rain, hung heavy in the air.

"Welcome," came a voice from deeper within.

The woman who emerged from the back looked as though she belonged in three centuries at once. She wore a long black dress, sleeves velvet at the cuffs, and a moss-green shawl wrapped around her shoulders. Her thick silver hair coiled like vines atop her head, and her storm cloud-gray eyes seemed to see everything at once — past, present, and maybe even what came next.

"I am glad to meet you," she said. "I felt that you were coming."

"How could you know?" Rachelle replied dryly.

The woman smiled, the corners of her eyes crinkling. "The universe knows; those who listen can learn."

They gathered near a round wooden table. It was

scarred by time and use, its surface set with mismatched teacups, each chipped in a different place. A velvet-lined tray of stones — moonstone, hematite, smoky quartz — rested at the center like forgotten treasure.

Charlotte stepped forward. "We came because someone said you know things. Things about…"

"Dark bargains," the woman finished. "Tethers. Old power. Places that breathe magic like lungs."

The group froze. She had named the very heart of it.

"Tea first," she said, already pouring from a pot that hadn't steamed a moment ago. "Nettle, clove, yarrow, and truthroot. Clears the vision. You'll need it."

She handed out cups — warm, mismatched, and fragile in their palms.

As they sipped, bitter and biting with heat, she watched them over her teacup like a hawk watching something squirm.

"Now," she said, "tell me what's haunting you."

They did. Each of them in turn.

Lucas spoke of the history he'd found buried online, old PDF scans and abandoned blogs full of local lore. Hudson recounted his late-night conversation with his grandmother, couched in hypotheticals, but heavy with warning. Rachelle and Alex described what they'd uncovered in the library archives: records of the land, deaths unexplained, pages missing. Charlotte shared her visit to the metaphysical store. The symbols she'd found. The way the air in the Annex changed when the magic stirred.

And finally, they told her about the woman. The locks of hair. The silent cost.

The old woman sat back, hands laced over the wide crystal pendant resting against her chest.

"That's no ghost," she said. "She's a bound witch. Baneful path, more than likely, she's made a dark bargain."

Lucas's voice was barely a whisper. "I... found that term online."

She gave a slow nod. "She traded her freedom for power or life. To keep it, she's tied herself to a ley point, deep under your school. A well of power, a gateway. Likely a convergence, where energy folds over itself like rivers beneath rock. Rare. But dangerous."

"She said we owed her," Alex added, voice tight. "For using her magic."

"She's not wrong, but it's not really hers," the woman said simply. "You dipped into the well. And now you will pay the toll, not fully sure to who."

Charlotte leaned forward, the teacup trembling slightly in her hand. "Can we break it?"

"That depends." The shopkeeper's voice dropped like a bell in still water. "She may be bound by an anchor spell. Or a geas. Or worse, regret. There are witches who cannot pass until the harm they did is healed. But she's broken now, yes? Hollow? The gateway will keep taking. It'll drain you until you're ash."

They all stared at the table. The stones glinted dully in the shifting light.

"What do we do?" Rachelle asked, barely audible.

The woman stood and crossed to a high shelf. She retrieved a small black box, a cloth sachet tied with thin red string, and a thin silver disk that swung from a chain like a moon caught in motion.

"Take these," she said. "Tourmaline and obsidian. Grounding stones. The herbs are for protection, rosemary, mugwort, vervain. Burn them, wear them, sleep with them. They remember what you forget."

Then she set the pendulum gently in the center of the table.

"For the truth. It knows what's hidden, if you let it."

Charlotte reached out, fingers closing around the cold silver chain.

The woman watched her a moment, then added, softly, "You'll want to find her true name. Not what she calls herself. Not what others call her. The name she never gave."

"Why?" Hudson asked.

"Because names are bindings. What is named is claimed. And what cannot be stolen... cannot be cursed."

She paused, letting the silence stretch.

"To cast it off," she said at last, voice slow and ritual-soft:

"Speak the truth aloud.

Not once, but thrice.

Beneath the full moon."

Stillness settled in the room. Heavy. Electric.

Then, unexpectedly, the woman leaned in, eyes softer now, and said:

"Not all witches bind. Not all witches bargain in blood. Most of us seek balance. We work with the land, with the wind and time. We weave harmony, not chains. Remember that when you meet her. She is not what we are. She chose another path."

Alex exhaled shakily. Charlotte nodded once. Rachelle's eyes glistened, but she blinked it back.

"We'll find the truth," Lucas said, firmer this time.

"You'd better," the woman replied, voice like wind in dry leaves. "Because you have till the next full moon... all dark bargains need the moon to seal the deal."

Her gaze cut through them, sharp and sorrowful all at once.

"Good luck little ones"

The bell above the tea shop door jingled softly as the five teens stepped back out into the fading afternoon sun. The light had shifted, longer shadows, softer edges, but everything still felt sharp in their chests. The woman's warnings echoed in all their heads, even as the scent of herbs and clove still clung to their clothes.

They stood at the bus stop quietly at first, not sure who should speak.

Finally, Charlotte pulled a mechanical pencil from her hoodie pocket and flipped to a clean page in her dotted notebook. "Okay. We need a plan."

Lucas gave a short laugh. "What, like an exorcism checklist?"

"No," Charlotte said. "A smart checklist."

"Smart?" Hudson asked.

"Specific. Measurable. Attainable. Realistic. Timely," she recited, already writing the words at the top of the page. "It's what my older sister used when she ran for student government. And if it works for crushing the student council, it can work for this."

Rachelle smirked. "I like this version of you."

Charlotte smiled faintly. "I like this version of me too."

Alex sat beside her on the bench, looking at the list over her shoulder as she began to scribble tasks:

1. Find Her True Name
2. Locate the Anchor Point in the Annex
3. Test Pendulum for Accuracy
4. Map the Ley Line or Power Source

5. Protective Gear (Sachets, Pendants, Salt,)
6. Research Full Moon Ritual Timing
7. Document everything - Journal, Drawings...

CHARLOTTE LOOKED UP. "Okay. Who's doing what?"

"I'll take the ley line map," Lucas said. "I already found the historic survey records online. It shouldn't be too hard to overlay that with the old blueprints we found."

I can test the pendulum," Rachelle said. "And prep the protection stuff. I still have most of the supplies from the tea shop."

I'll help with the anchor point," Hudson said. "I remember where the floors felt weird in the Annex. Like... hollow."

Charlotte looked at Alex. "You and me on name duty?"

He nodded. "Yeah. I'll check the library for anything weird about staff records or faculty stories, there has to be something."

Charlotte tapped the pencil against her lip. "And I'll try to find any symbols or old language stuff. If she was ever written about or sealed, maybe someone left a clue."

The bus hissed up to the curb, and they climbed on in a quiet line. The driver barely looked up as they filed into the back and collapsed into the same corner bench they always did.

They sat shoulder to shoulder now, not just as friends, but as something deeper. A crew. A circle. A secret.

Charlotte closed her notebook.

"Well," she said, "looks like we all know what we're doing."

"But we also know where we have to go next," Alex added. "The Annex. It's where everything ties together."

Lucas blew out a breath. "Monday morning then?"

"Before the gates open," Rachelle confirmed.

"No turning back this time," Hudson said.

Charlotte met each of their eyes in turn.

"We've already given pieces of ourselves. Might as well see what those pieces can unlock."

As the bus trundled toward home, their destination was set.

Monday morning.

The Annex.

The truth.

Whatever it cost.

On Sunday night Alex headed out to his porch. The

porch light buzzed softly overhead as Alex pushed open the front door. The sun had already dipped below the horizon, leaving streaks of orange and violet behind it.

The street was quiet, just the occasional bark of a dog or the hum of a passing car.

Rachelle was already waiting on the porch swing, one leg tucked underneath her, sipping from a bottle of water. Charlotte arrived moments later, bike helmet still hanging from her handlebars. She dropped it onto the porch with a soft clatter and sat on the opposite side of the swing.

Alex settled across from them on the wooden box, arms draped casually over his knees.

For a moment, none of them said anything. The night was still, and so were they.

Rachelle broke the silence. "I didn't think this would get so real."

Charlotte gave a soft, humorless laugh. "I thought this would be some secret club. Like... magic tricks and floating pencils. Not being locked to a well for the rest of our lives."

Alex looked down at his hands, voice low. "I keep thinking... this all started with me."

The girls turned toward him.

"I picked the lock," he said. "I went in first. I brought you, Rachelle. Then Lucas and Hudson. Then Charlotte. I pulled everyone in. And now we're all... tied to her."

"Alex..." Rachelle began, but he shook his head.

"I can't stop thinking about it," he said, voice tight. "If I had just left that chain alone, if I hadn't gotten obsessed with that padlock... maybe none of this would've happened. You'd both be safe. Free. But, I was drawn to it. I can't explain it better than that."

Rachelle shifted off the swing and sat beside him on the step. "You think I wouldn't have gone in? You think I would've let you face that alone?"

Alex stared ahead. "I didn't think it'd matter. I didn't know what I was messing with."

"None of us did," Charlotte said quietly, moving closer on the other side. "You didn't drag me in, Alex. I chose this. I wanted to be part of this. I practically begged for it."

"Yeah," Rachelle said, "and honestly? If we hadn't found this... we'd still be stuck in boring classes, pretending nothing big ever happens. At least now we know the truth."

Charlotte gave a soft smile. "Scary as it is... I'd rather be scared with you two than bored with anyone else."

Alex exhaled slowly. "I just... I can't lose either of you. Not because I made a stupid choice."

"You didn't," Rachelle said firmly. "You made a brave one."

Charlotte reached out and linked her hand with Alex's. "We're already in this, all of us. But the best part is... we're not alone."

Rachelle reached across and added her hand, their fingers all linked in the glow of the porch light.

It was warm there. Not safe. Not certain. But solid.

"I'm still scared," Charlotte whispered.

"Me too," Rachelle said.

Alex nodded, squeezing their hands. "But at least we're scared together."

10

ARMED WITH INFORMATION

The five teens stepped through the gate and up the steps into the front entrance. Alex picked up the pace, feeling the urgency. Rachelle and Charlotte watched for anyone in the halls. They slipped down the long, cold corridor heading toward the Annex.

Once inside, Alex led the way with his flashlight beam cutting a narrow tunnel through the dark. They were quieter than usual this morning — no joking, no excited whispers, just the shared silence of kids carrying too many thoughts at once.

Rachelle was the one who finally spoke, her voice soft and dry. "This still feels wrong."

Charlotte didn't answer. She was too busy scanning

the walls, the corners, the ceilings, anywhere that might hold a symbol, a marking, anything missed before.

They passed through the hallway of the Annex, and just like always, the warmth greeted them first. Not comforting warmth, this heat clung to their skin like breath, too warm for stone, too alive for an abandoned building.

They didn't go to the large central room right away. This time, they turned down one of the unexplored corridors, toward a wing partially blocked by fallen timber and rusted support beams.

But the jar still waited.

It sat on the low stone pedestal where they'd left it last time, its glass murky, the swirling strands of hair inside faintly glowing. Something old and wrong shimmered around it.

"I'm going to try it," Hudson said, stepping forward. He squared his shoulders and braced his hands on the jar.

As soon as his fingers touched it, his arms jolted back as if he'd been zapped. "Whoa!"

Alex caught him before he stumbled.

Hudson's face scrunched. "It's like it's glued to the air."

"No," Charlotte murmured, crouching low beside it. "It's not a physical binding. It's warded."

"What does that mean?" Lucas asked.

Charlotte pointed to the base of the pedestal. Her finger traced several faint, curling lines, hidden unless you were looking. "It means she didn't just plant it here. She sealed it. Like... magically cemented. With intent."

Charlotte showed him her note about warding. "I think this is what it is."

They spent the next hour carefully exploring parts of the Annex they had not dared venture into yet. An old art room with overturned metal tables. A workshop full of rusted tools and broken shelving. One room with walls covered entirely in cracked mirrors, some reflecting only darkness, no matter how close they stood.

No one had used their powers since the pact. They were afraid using them would be felt and be answered with a feeding. Since the air had gone cold and the witch had whispered over that black-glass jar like it was listening, it had not felt right.

The memory of it lingered — cold, sticky, wrong. A pact sealed with pieces of themselves.

So they avoided it. Avoid that.

Except Lucas.

He stepped forward into the center of the room, the old gym-theater hybrid in the basement of the annex. The space where they had first tried to understand what was happening to them. Where things had cracked open in more ways than one.

"Okay," he said, clearing his throat. "Just one thing. I'm not using anything. Not really. Just... showing something."

His voice was lighter than usual, but not flippant. He looked at the others as if asking for permission without saying it.

Alex watched him but said nothing. Rachelle shrugged one shoulder. Hudson folded his arms, eyes wary but not objecting. Charlotte nodded once, barely perceptibly.

With a flick of Lucas's hand, the air shimmered.

Like watercolor soaking into paper, the dingy space began to change.

Light trickled into corners where none should have reached, soft and golden, as if filtered through cathedral windows. The cracked tile floor gleamed suddenly, flawless, and opalescent, like freshly polished marble reflecting some unseen sun.

The ceiling rose above them, much higher than physics could allow, and curved into a dome painted with whorls of sapphire and lavender clouds. Hidden stars glittered behind layers of illusory mist.

Columns sprouted up from the sides of the room, twisting, carved with vines and strange creatures that blinked and curled their tails as if just waking from stone.

The air warmed. A gentle breeze swept across their faces, carrying the scent of blooming jasmine and something more ancient, like parchment and cedarwood.

From somewhere above, birdsong echoed softly. And the distant chime of bells, soft, melodic, like wind in a glass forest.

Charlotte drew in a slow breath, her eyes wide. "Lucas..." she said, barely above a whisper. "This is... beautiful."

Lucas gave a lopsided smile, his usual smirk subdued into something more vulnerable. "I figured we needed to see this place as something else. Just once. Not cursed. Not haunted. Just... ours. Even if it's fake."

Rachelle turned in a slow circle, eyes tracing the painted sky. "It doesn't feel fake."

"It feels like it remembers," Alex murmured, staring up.

Hudson rubbed his arm, but even he allowed a quiet, grudging, "Not bad, Bruh."

Lucas glanced toward the jar, just briefly. His illusion didn't touch it. He left it sitting there in shadow, untouched by magic or light.

"I didn't use anything new," he said. "Didn't take. Just... reshaped what was already here."

"We know," Charlotte said. She reached out and touched one of the shimmering columns. Her fingers passed through it, but gently, like brushing a sunbeam.

They stood there for a while longer, quiet in the warmth. Wrapped in it.

None of them said it aloud, but they were grateful. Grateful to see the place as it could be, not broken and cold, but bright. A memory of what might still be possible.

Eventually, the illusion began to thin. First the bird-song faded, then the scent of jasmine, then the shimmer peeled back from the walls like mist burning away at dawn.

Above them, the ceiling shrank. The cracks in the floor returned. The light dimmed.

Somewhere beyond the walls, footsteps echoed; the school was waking up.

Rachelle sighed. "Time to be normal again."

Charlotte didn't move, not right away. "Just a little longer."

Lucas nodded. "Yeah. Just a little."

And they stayed, even after the illusion was gone, as if its warmth had seeped into their bones.

They crowded into the back corner of the cafeteria, hunched around a table with their food mostly untouched.

Alex unfolded a sheet of paper he had carefully

folded into quarters. Charlotte had copied several of the runes, and a translated phrase across the top.

"We think her name was Molga," Alex said.

Hudson frowned. "Sounds like an elf from a fantasy game."

Rachelle leaned in. "We found it in old land records. She lived where the school is now. Her entire family died mysteriously. She stayed... and she never left."

Amanda walked by, sneering at Charlotte. "Trash."

Rachelle leaped over the table, pushing Amanda back a few steps. Hudson was up quickly, holding her back, and waving off Amanda.

"We need to be under the radar right now," Alex said with a smile at Rachelle's arms and legs flailing as strong Hudson held her.

"You're definitely fire." Hudson said.

That got a chuckle out of Lucas, who saw the same thing.

"It's just that we are dealing with life and death and we don't have time for her crap." Rachelle retorted. "Her petty nonsense pisses me off!"

Charlotte gave a smile of acknowledgement to Rachelle, understanding completely how she was feeling. "Thank you."

Charlotte motioned them to come closer. "I found symbols tied to a spell called The Binding Wheel. It's used to root a witch's soul to a place. And based on what's warding the jar, she used something powerful. Personal. A lock of hair. A name. Something sacred."

Lucas nodded slowly. "And if that name still has power..."

"It might be how we undo the deal," Alex finished. "Or at least loosen it."

They all looked at each other.

For the first time since they'd entered the Annex, there was a flicker of hope.

But Rachelle voiced the thought on everyone's mind: "If her name has power... whose hands does that put us in?"

No one answered. Because they all knew the answer. Theirs. Or hers. Or whoever had trapped her.

The final bell echoed across the campus like a warning. Students spilled into the halls, laughing, shoving, slamming lockers shut, but none of that touched the five teens clustered near the old vending machine behind the gym. They barely spoke as they waited for the stragglers to pass, the noise of the day bleeding away around them.

Alex looked at his friends in turn. "Tomorrow morning. We go in, and we use her name."

Charlotte glanced around, then lowered her voice. "And if it doesn't work?"

Rachelle didn't blink. "Then we'll find another way."

"Carefully," Lucas added, but his tone carried the

weight of fear beneath the joke. "I'd really prefer not to be fed on this week."

Hudson cracked his knuckles, then crossed his arms. "We can handle her. She's old. And pissed. But she's not invincible."

They agreed quietly and collectively: In the morning, they would confront Molga. But none of them slept well.

It was Charlotte who woke up first, if it could be called waking. Her body never moved. But her mind snapped into cold, crystalline clarity, as if someone had turned on the lights inside her own head.

She was standing in the Annex.

Alone.

And Molga was waiting.

Her presence didn't enter the room. It became the room. The walls bled warmth; the floor pulsed faintly like breathing earth. Shadows curled into corners where they didn't belong.

Charlotte tried to move, but her limbs felt heavy, like they'd been buried in stone.

Molga stepped forward, or something like her did.

Her eyes were colorless. Not white or black, just the absence of all color, like scraped-out porcelain. Her hair floated around her like slow smoke, and when she smiled, it was all bone and bitter memory.

"You came lured into my trap," she said.

"You played with power."

"You will feed the beast."

Charlotte opened her mouth to speak, but her voice was gone. Molga leaned close, too close.

"And now... you think my name belongs to you? He watches you, he's coming for you. "

Then she vanished, and Charlotte bolted upright in bed, gasping. Her cheeks were soaked with tears.

Rachelle found herself in the Annex's central chamber, but it was burning, the walls curling in heat, embers dancing in the air like fireflies.

Her hands lit with flame... but flickered out.

Again and again, she summoned fire, but the flames fizzled. Cold fire. Hollow fire.

A voice rose behind her.

"Your flame is taken."

Molga appeared barefoot on scorched tiles, her feet leaving no ash. Her hair streamed behind her like smoke, her face young and ancient all at once.

"Did you think the fire was yours?"

"You burned the air, the ground. You lit your soul with a match you didn't strike."

Rachelle backed up.

Molga stepped closer.

"Try again, girl. Try to burn me."

Rachelle screamed and raised her hand, and nothing happened.

"Run, girl, he is coming," Molga hissed, her breath like ice. "Next time, you may not make it out."

Lucas was in a throne room, a grand illusion he recognized from his own magic. Stained glass poured rainbow light across the floor, and velvet banners flapped above.

He was the king of illusion.

Then the glass cracked. The banners turned to rags. The air twisted.

Molga walked through the throne like it was mist. His illusion peeled away around her with every step.

"I see what's real, Lucas. I always see."

"You cloak your fears in beauty. You spin lies to hide the truth. But you can't fool me."

Lucas fell to the ground, clutching his temples. His illusions screamed as they died.

"Even as you use it, the more he sees you," she whispered. "And you have so much to take already."

"He sees you."

Hudson stood before a brick wall, the same wall he'd once lifted in the Annex. It loomed twice as tall now, casting a heavy shadow.

He reached to move it again, confident.

But the brick crumbled in his hands, revealing bones beneath.

His family's bones. His friends'. All hollowed out.

Molga stood behind him, cloaked in earth and dust, her fingers trailing through broken mortar.

"You think your strength makes you safe?"

"You'll carry the weight of everyone you love. One day, you'll drop them."

"Do not try to shoulder this burden."

Hudson dropped to his knees, the wall pressing down, heavy, suffocating.

Molga knelt beside him.

"Do not try, strong boy. He will break you."

Alex was back in the Annex.

The jar floated in midair, glowing, humming. One by one, his friends stood around it, silent. Their hair floated out of their heads and into the jar. When it was his turn, Alex tried to resist, but his own fingers reached up, plucking a strand and dropping it in.

He screamed.

Molga's hand clamped over his mouth.

"You brought them here."

"You opened the door. Let them in. Gave them magic. Showed them my name."

Her eyes bore into his. Not angry, knowing.

"You were the key. You are the hinge. And when it closes, when it breaks, it will be on you."

She traced a finger down his cheek.

"He played you. If you care about what happens to the ones you love, run."

He woke up drenched in sweat.

When they gathered before school, no one said they had a dream.

But they all knew.

One glance at each other's faces, pale, drawn, eyes ringed with exhaustion, told them everything.

Molga had visited all of them.

And she had one single warning:

Get out.

She said the same thing to all of them, in different words, but the meaning was identical: "This is his place. You are in my place now. Run away."

Charlotte was the first to say it. "She saw us."

"She was in my head," Lucas said. "It felt like she peeled it open."

Rachelle nodded, pale. "Mine too."

Alex's fists clenched. "She knows what we're planning."

Hudson's voice was flat. "She warned us to try to get away."

They all stared at each other, the weight of her warning sinking in.

But no one said the one thing they were all thinking: *Are we going to do it anyway? Are we ready?*

The garden behind the gym, once part of the school's old landscaping plans, had gone mostly forgotten, overgrown with lavender, ivy, and dry soil beds. But it was quiet, shaded, and just far enough from foot traffic that no one would interrupt.

Charlotte spread a folded piece of graph paper across the bench as if it was sacred. "Okay," she said, smoothing it down, "let's go over what we actually know."

They all huddled closer — Alex, Rachelle, Hudson, and Lucas. Tired eyes. Tense shoulders. But committed.

Charlotte pointed to the top of the page.

"Molga" — probable name of the witch bound beneath the school.

"Lived on this land in the 1700s. Her entire family died. No cause of death listed. There is no record of her leaving."

Alex rubbed his hands together, nerves getting the better of him. "And now she's trapped in the Annex. Or under it. Or through it."

"Or all three," Lucas muttered.

Rachelle exhaled sharply. "And we woke her up."

There was a beat of silence.

Hudson finally said what none of them wanted to: "She was in our dreams. She saw us. She knows us."

Charlotte glanced at Alex. "Say it again. The spell. The name."

Alex hesitated, then repeated softly: "Molga Ruen. It was written in old runes on the wall behind the jar. Charlotte figured it out."

"I didn't figure it," Charlotte said. "It was like it was waiting to be read."

Rachelle leaned forward. "Are we sure that's her name and not just another title? We use it, and then what? We free her?"

"Or seal her again?" Lucas offered.

Charlotte shook her head. "She was sealed before. This time... maybe we don't fight her. Maybe we try to understand her."

Alex looked at her. "Even after what she said?"

"She's afraid," Charlotte said. "Of something. Of someone. Or regrets, I don't know; I just feel something is not right."

Hudson clenched his fists. "She threatened us."

"She warned us," Rachelle corrected. "There's a difference."

Lucas drummed his fingers on the bench. "So we're going back in tomorrow. What's our move?"

Charlotte flipped to the next page. She'd written tasks:

Re-read the inscription near the jar.
Attempt a protection circle, use tourmaline, obsidian, salt line.
Try to communicate, not challenge.
See if the jar responds to her name.

Look for more runes, markings, or contracts.

"We go in calm," Charlotte said. "No spells. No fighting. No showing off. Just observation and contact."

Rachelle gave Alex a long look. "Are you okay with that?"

Alex nodded. "I got us into this. I'm not walking away now."

Hudson gave him a fist bump, then stood. "Then tomorrow, we go back into the Annex. Prepared."

Lucas laughed nervously. "You know, there's still time to fake sick and drop out."

"No, there's not," Charlotte said, folding the paper. "This is our story now."

They stood together in the fading light, the wind shifting through the dry garden leaves.

And in the silence that followed, none of them said the fear out loud, but they all felt it.

Tomorrow, they would confront Molga.

And she would be waiting.

They stepped through the Annex doors together, the heavy silence swallowing their footsteps. It smelled of old dust and charred wood, like a memory burned too many times to fade. The walls still bore the marks

— runes half-scrawled in ash, shadows that didn't quite move when you blinked.

Charlotte clutched the satchel the shopkeeper had given her. The faint scent of mugwort and rosemary lingered on her wrist. The pendulum dangled from her other hand, twitching softly, like it knew what was coming.

"We stick to the plan," Alex said, his voice barely above a whisper. "Talk first. Understand her. No powers unless we have to."

They found her in the atrium, the heart of the Annex. Molga stood beneath the cracked skylight, a broken halo of light cutting across her face. Her eyes flickered with something too deep and old to name. The shadows clung to her like armor.

"So," she said. Her voice rippled across the room like the first hiss of wind before a storm. "You came back."

"We came to talk," Charlotte said, stepping forward. Her voice was steady, though her hands trembled. "We want to understand you. To help you... if that's still possible."

Molga tilted her head. "Why would I want your help?"

"Because you're bound here," Alex said. "Not by someone else. Of your own free will. We know. You tied yourself to the power in this place."

The air in the Annex thickened. Rachelle could feel the temperature drop, the kind of cold that slid under your skin.

"I chose this?" Molga said. "My family... gone to give me life. My name... forgotten for protection. But this land remembers me. The ley line sings beneath it, and I am its echo."

"You don't have to be," Hudson said. "There's still time to let go."

Molga's smile was like cracked porcelain. "Time? You children speak of time as if you understand what it means to watch the world spin without you. To be nothing but the hunger left behind."

Without warning, the room erupted.

Books flew from shelves. Desks overturned. lights flickered. A rusted light fixture shrieked loose from the ceiling and hurled itself toward them.

Charlotte threw up both hands. A golden shield flared into existence around them, shimmering like glass in sunlight. The chandelier crashed against it and shattered, sparks flying.

"Enough!" Alex shouted. He stepped forward, lifting one hand.

Molga began to rise. Her feet left the floor, hair and cloak twisting as if underwater.

She hissed. "You dare..."

"Yes, I dare, for the second you fed my friends to some dark beast, it became personal!" Alex growled.

Rachelle's palms lit with flame, blue at the edges. "We gave you a chance; we wanted to understand," she said. "But now take this as our answer."

She let loose a volley, three bolts of fire streaking toward Molga. They struck her squarely in the chest, the impact knocking her back. Her arms whipped above her head, but she laughed, the sound dry and sharp like broken teeth.

"You don't understand!" she shrieked. "Use the power, he feeds all the same! The more you burn, the deeper your roots grow. This is his garden now, my bargain, but his harvest!"

Alex felt it then, a tug in his chest. Like something inside him being siphoned, bled out thread by thread. Rachelle gasped beside him, swaying.

"Something's feeding off the magic," Lucas warned. "She wants us to fight."

"Then stop!" Hudson cried. "If we don't win by overpowering her. Maybe we win by starving them."

Charlotte dropped her shield. Alex let Molga fall. Rachelle doused her flame.

Molga dropped to the floor with a snarl, staggering.

"No, nothing has changed," she rasped. "You are still tethered."

"What do we owe you?" Charlotte asked. "You

chained yourself here. You chose this loneliness. You don't owe me; you owe him."

Alex stepped forward, steady now. "But we'll give you what no one else ever did."

Molga looked up, trembling.

"A chance," he said. "To be free."

Charlotte held out the pendulum, now glowing with a pale light. "Let us find it. Let us free you."

The witch stared at them, hollow-eyed and shaking.

And for the first time...

She didn't laugh.

They didn't speak much on the walk home after school.

The wind carried the smell of cut grass and far away rain, but none of them noticed. Their bodies were tired; worse, their spirits were stretched thin, like threads too close to snapping.

Alex's hoodie clung damply to his back. Lucas rubbed his temples. Rachelle didn't even pull out a snack. Hudson kept clenching and unclenching his fists like he couldn't decide whether to punch something or pray. And Charlotte, always the composed one, stared so hard at the horizon it looked like she was trying to read something only she could see.

They ended up in Hudson's backyard. It was quiet there, tucked behind a chain-link fence, the smell of lemon balm rising from his grandma's herb patch. A string of warm bulbs flickered on above the patio.

They collapsed into mismatched lawn chairs.

No one spoke for a full minute.

Then Rachelle broke the silence.

"She laughed when I hit her with fire." Her voice was hollow. "She liked it."

Charlotte nodded grimly. "She's not just feeding off our magic. She's dependent on it. That whole outburst — it was bait."

Hudson leaned forward. "We almost gave her exactly what she wanted."

"We did," Alex muttered, head in his hands. "We used our powers. We fed her."

"You didn't know," Rachelle said gently.

Alex lowered his eyes, "but I should've. I got us into this. I pushed us into the Annex in the first place."

"No," Charlotte said. "We all chose to go. We all said yes."

Lucas looked up from his phone. "I've been rereading everything. Soul-binding, leyline anchors, old-world witchcraft. There are no easy outs. But there are patterns."

Charlotte nodded. "She didn't react when I mentioned names."

"That's the key," Lucas said. "The pendulum glowed. True names have power."

"So we find it," Hudson said. "Her real name. Not Molga. Not the title she made up for herself."

Alex looked over at Charlotte. "What's our next move?"

She took a breath, grounding herself. Then she reached into her bag and pulled out her notebook. She flipped past drawings, copied symbols, pressed petals.

"We split the work," she said. "Again."

She pointed to Hudson. "Your grandma, ask her about the original families who lived on the land. Any stories passed down. Even whispers."

"To me?" Hudson raised a brow.

"She talks to you. And she knows things. Try."

Charlotte turned to Lucas. "Library archives again. Dig deeper. Check old property records, birth and death certificates, anything with names connected to the land."

Lucas nodded, already texting himself reminders.

"We should all go back to the tea shop," Charlotte added. "The woman there might know older naming rituals. Especially for witches who've masked themselves."

Alex swallowed. "What about me?"

Charlotte answered before Rachelle could. "You come with me. We've still got the map of the leyline under the school. If we find the exact spot where she anchored herself, maybe we can weaken her."

Charlotte looked at them all. "This time, we don't fight. We don't flare. We don't feed her."

Lucas gave a dry chuckle. "So, detective mode?"

"Exactly," Alex said. "We find her name. Then we end this."

The porch lights buzzed overhead. Somewhere across the street, a dog barked once, then fell silent.

They sat there for a while, letting the plan settle around them like armor. Bruised. Scared. But not broken.

Tomorrow, they'd dig into the past. Tonight, they'd rest. Because next time... They weren't going in blind.

After school they take the bus back to the little shop. The bell over the shop door chimed like a distant wind chime caught in memory. The group stepped into Tea & Truth again, the scent of clove and roots already steeped in their clothes like ghost perfume. A storm brewed somewhere on the edge of the day, the light outside faded gray and golden, but inside the shop, everything was still, timeless.

The old shopkeeper was at her usual place, hunched over a tea tray with her sleeves rolled to her elbows, her silver hair wound in a loose knot that shimmered with a life of its own.

"I hoped you'd return," she said, not looking up. "I felt a ripple last night. She reached for your dreams."

Charlotte stepped forward. Her notebook was

clutched to her chest, a few pages sticking out where she'd scribbled furiously during their research binge. "We think we found her name. Her real one."

At that, the woman finally looked up. Her storm-gray eyes sharpened.

"Speak it," she said.

Alex shifted nervously. "Molga. We think... Molga Ruen was her name even before she died. Before she became what she is."

The woman's hands froze over the tray. Then slowly, she lowered them.

"Molga. That poor child never had a chance," she said. "I've not heard that name aloud in decades."

They stared, quiet.

Charlotte asked, "You know her?"

"I know of her," the woman corrected. "It is one of the oldest legends of this region. She lived before the town existed. She was born of pain. Her father has killed working the field, fever took her mother and her siblings. She lived alone on cursed land, the same land the school is on now. The leyline breathed beneath her, and instead of healing, she made it her tethered. She wasn't always cruel, but grief... grief twists even gentle hands."

Lucas cleared his throat. "Why?"

"Legend is she made a deal with a demon." the old woman shivered. "If you went to the ley, or even near it, he knows of you. Can you feel it. Do you sense he watches you."

Hudson let out a low whistle. "So we're not just dealing with the ghost of a witch. Some demon is hunting us too."

The shopkeeper nodded. "And you are feeding him."

They all feel the slight tug at their hearts. Charlotte put her hand over hers, Alex nodding he feels it too.

"He's getting stronger now that he has all of you to feed on," the woman added. "And I can see he has begun harvesting your life, so the contract is already deep."

Rachelle stepped forward. "We didn't know what we were agreeing to. Is there any way to break it?"

The woman moved behind the counter and opened a tall, dust-smudged cupboard. From within, she retrieved a faded cloth bundle tied with black twine. She laid it on the table and carefully unwrapped it. Inside were parchment scrolls, aged herbs, and a thin glass vial filled with something glowing faintly blue.

"There may be a way, I am not even sure this will work at this point," she said. "But a reversal spell may be able to undo the pact. It's Rare. And it can be danger-ous. This could be you only hope."

Charlotte leaned closer. "What does it do?"

"I theory, it could unwind the soul-tether. Pulls back

what was taken. But it has to be done at the source, her anchor point. You must speak her name, her true name, with intent, three times. Then break the contract. And offer a sacrifice."

Lucas frowned. "What kind of sacrifice?"

The woman gave him a look so old it quieted the room.

"You'll know when the moment comes," she said softly. "Magic doesn't take without giving. You want your lives back... something else must be offered."

The group exchanged uneasy glances.

Charlotte asked, "What if it doesn't work?"

"Then he claims you. Over time he'll feed. Maybe slowly. Year by year. Dream by dream."

Hudson crossed his arms. "We're going to need more than tea and crystals for this."

The shopkeeper smiled faintly. "Yeah, that is an understatement."

She handed each of them a different pouch, tea infused with symbols, powdery herbs, a thumb-sized charm. "Protection," she said. "Focus. Courage. And truth."

Alex took his with a small nod. "Thank you."

"You've taken the first step," she said. "That's more than most."

Charlotte turned back before they left. "Why help us?"

The woman looked at her with eyes that saw through time.

"Because not all witches want to take," she said gently. "most of us only wish to mend."

The wind had picked up outside. The hanging sign squeaked again. There was a storm coming.

They stepped into the waning light, spell kits tucked under arms and hearts a little heavier, but clearer.

Molga Ruen, they know her name now, at least they were pretty sure.

And that name had power.

11

LOOKING FOR THE LEY

Charlotte and Alex blinked softly at their screens late into the night. Most of the group chat had gone quiet, except for them.

Alex:

we have to find the ley point

before anything else happens

Charlotte:

agreed

just us?

Alex:

i need to do this

i got us into it

Charlotte:

then I'm going with you

I can shield us

and i'm brave enough to drag you out

Alex:

meet me early?

side of the school. 6:00

Charlotte:

don't make me regret this

The air was crisp and still as Charlotte met Alex in the dim pre-dawn near the edge of the school grounds. The grass was wet; the light golden where it broke through the fog. They didn't speak much as they slipped through the fence, moving with practiced steps, through the front entrance, toward the forgotten annex.

Alex carried the pendulum around his neck, its silver disk swaying faintly, already beginning to shimmer.

Inside, the annex was colder than it should've been, the quiet pressing on their skin like silk-wrapped lead. Their footsteps barely echoed, almost as if the building didn't want them to be noticed.

"Where do we start?" Charlotte whispered.

Alex pulled out the pendant, holding it flat in his palm. The stone vibrated faintly, pulsing with a soft inner glow. "We follow the pull."

They moved slowly through twisting halls and forgotten doorways, the pendant swinging like a compass. Shadows crawled at the edge of their vision, but they didn't use magic, just stayed close. Closer than they ever had before. When Charlotte's hand brushed Alex's, she didn't pull away. Instead, she laced her fingers into his.

He didn't breathe for a moment. Her hand was warm and steady.

Finally, at the far end of a boarded hallway, behind a half-collapsed door, they found it.

Buried by a circle of debris, a ruined shaft under the now broken floor. Alex levitated all the debris, revealing below a stone lined, cracked and worn, long forgotten. Roots curled through it like fingers clutching from below. The pendant pulsed a vibrant blue, the glow spilling onto their hands, their faces, like moonlight underwater.

Charlotte stepped closer, her voice barely audible. "It's beautiful."

Alex could barely speak. "It's alive."

They stood there in silent awe, their hands still

joined. He could feel the rhythm of her breath. The warmth of her courage.

"This is it," he whispered. "The ley point. This is where she anchored herself."

Charlotte gave a tight nod. "Then we know where to break the tether."

They turned together, still hand in hand, following their steps back through the hush of the annex. The door loomed ahead, gray morning light spilling through the cracks.

Just before they reached it, the threshold of the Annex, the familiar door that always felt like the edge of something deeper, Charlotte pulled gently on Alex's hand.

Her fingers brushed him, the warmth of his arm on her fingertips. He stopped, turning to her with a quiet question in his eyes, brows raised.

Charlotte didn't answer with words.

She stepped in, close enough to feel the soft rise of his breath against her skin, and kissed him.

It wasn't hurried. It wasn't dramatic.

It was careful. Brave. Real.

Her lips met his, warm and soft, tasting faintly of the gum he always chewed when he was nervous. His breath caught, just a little, like she'd pulled him out of gravity. The same way he had made her weightless. She felt his hand rise slowly, hesitantly, then rest on her waist, light, like he didn't want to startle her.

Her own hand curled near his collarbone, fingers resting over the steady rhythm of his heartbeat.

The world fell away to just that, his touch, his breath, the scent of him. Clean laundry. Rain on pavement. As the kiss deepened, they lifted off the ground, surrounded by a golden orb of shielding. They held on to each other feeling nothing but each other, but it felt like an entire conversation passed between them, unspoken but understood.

When she finally pulled back her lips, she hovered there for a moment, close enough to feel the whisper of air between them. Her eyes searched his face, and her voice came out soft and certain, barely a breath: "I just wanted you to know."

Alex didn't say anything at first, as they touched down. His eyes lingered on her lips, then lifted to meet hers. One hand still rested at her side, the other now at the small of her back like he didn't want to let the moment drift.

Then he smiled, pulling her into a hug.

A little stunned.

"I know," he said. "I really do."

Charlotte felt the warmth rise in her cheeks, but she didn't pull away.

For the first time in what felt like forever, the buzz in her chest wasn't fear or uncertainty. It was light. It was hope.

And maybe... the start of something she hadn't dared let herself want until now.

"We see the end of the tunnel; we are almost free."

Alex didn't move for a heartbeat. His world had changed in an instant. All the fear, all the tension, every ounce of guilt and weight in his chest, melted.

He smiled. That was the most amazing thing that had ever happened to him.

Charlotte raised an eyebrow, already halfway through the door. "Let's save our friends."

And together, they stepped back into the light. Too late to meet the others before class.

MR. WILLY'S voice droned on about the westward expansion, but Alex's mind was nowhere near the early 1800s.

From his spot two rows behind Rachelle, he glanced sideways, first to Rachelle, then back to the notebook in front of him. He tapped his pen three times, then two taps, then one tap.

"Pay attention."

Rachelle's eyes flicked up from her notes. She

nodded almost imperceptibly, brushing her thumb along the edge of her desk — a return signal.

"Watching."

Alex lifted his hand and held one finger up.

"I have something to tell."

He angled his notebook slightly, as if adjusting it, then dragged his finger across the spiral binding.

"Big. Important."

Across the room, Hudson caught the movement. He raised his left eyebrow and rolled his pen in his fingers three times.

"Now?"

Alex tapped his thumb on the desk twice.

"No. Later."

Charlotte, sitting diagonally in front of him, had already noticed the silent exchange. She brushed her hair behind her ear and nodded when their eyes met.

Lucas, late as usual and scribbling something that looked suspiciously like dungeon schematics instead of notes, finally noticed the ripple of eye contact and fingers twitching. Alex made a quick motion, scratching his neck with two fingers.

"After second period."

Lucas gave a tiny salute with his pencil.

Mr. Willy turned from the whiteboard, and the signals stopped instantly. The whole group dropped back into fake note-taking postures, just as he said, "And what do we think that tells us about early American expansion?"

No one answered.

But Alex smiled quietly to himself.

They'd meet. After second period.

THE BELL RANG, ending the second period, sending a river of students flooding the halls of Westridge High. In the middle of it all, Alex and Charlotte stood just outside the science wing, barely paying attention to the crowd. They had walked in together that morning, and anyone paying close enough attention would've noticed how they stood closer than usual. How they kept glancing at each other with unspoken energy humming between them.

"We have to tell the others," Alex said quietly, checking to make sure no one nearby was listening. |

Charlotte nodded. "At lunch. All of it."

Her eyes met his, and for a second they both remembered the kiss, the soft blue glow of the ley point still imprinted in their minds like a secret tattoo.

"Not all of it," he gave a crooked smile.

They spotted Lucas first, thumbing at his phone near his locker.

"You found it?" he asked, voice dropping. His eyebrows shot up as Charlotte nodded. "Where?"

"We'll explain everything," Alex said. "At lunch. Our Table?"

"Lunch," Lucas echoed.

By the time the bell rang for third period, Hudson and Rachelle had been quietly told, and the group was set. But something flickered behind Rachelle's expression. She smiled, but her eyes didn't.

Alex didn't notice. Charlotte did.

The group met for lunch. 12:01 PM. Their table was perfect for privacy, tucked in the back corner.

Alex began, "The ley point is real. We found it. Under the annex, past the boarded corridor. It's covered in debris, but the pendant glowed as if it was responding to it."

"You're sure it's the point?" Hudson asked, arms crossed.

Charlotte nodded. "Positive. You could feel it. Like... like your whole body was listening."

"That's where she's tied," Alex added. "Her anchor."

Rachelle sat across from Alex, her arms folded tight across her chest. She looked at Charlotte, then Alex. "You went together, just the two of you?"

Alex turned a little slowly. "Yeah. It felt safer, just the two of us. Quieter."

Rachelle's jaw twitched. She masked it quickly. "Right. Makes sense, but we would have come."

Lucas, oblivious, scribbled ideas on his notepad. "So if the anchor is there, maybe the reversal spell the tea lady mentioned has to be performed at the ley point. While she is distracted or weakened."

"She's may resist, she is under another's control," Hudson said flatly. "We need to be ready for anything."

Charlotte adjusted the pendant on her necklace. "That's why we need a plan. Not just magic, but timing, protection, strategy."

Alex nodded. "We meet tonight. Go over everything. Assign roles. And... we don't use her magic again unless we absolutely have to. No more fuel for her."

Everyone nodded slowly. Even Rachelle.

But when Charlotte leaned over to whisper something to Alex, Rachelle could sense something had changed.

The sun hung low, burning orange through the slats of Lucas's bedroom blinds. His game room, usually scattered with dice, game controllers, and half-finished soda cans, had been transformed into a war room. The TV was off. The consoles were unplugged. A whiteboard stood in the corner, scribbled over in marker: timelines, symbols, possible outcomes, and in the middle, Saturday circled in red three times.

Lucas sat cross-legged on the carpet, shuffling index

cards like playing cards, each one labeled: Diversion, Distraction, Containment, Exit Plan.

"We go on Saturday," Charlotte said, perched on the arm of a sagging beanbag. "It's the only time we're guaranteed not to be interrupted."

"And we can stay as long as we need," Hudson added. "No classes. No teachers."

"Or suspicious parents," Rachelle said under her breath. She sat near the window, watching the last sunlight catch in the trees outside.

Alex stood by the whiteboard, arms folded. His brows were drawn tight, but there was clarity in his voice. "We need three things: one, to keep from being fed on. Two, get to the ley point and perform the reversal. Three..." He hesitated. "Survive."

Silence settled in like dust.

Charlotte broke it. "We'll need protection spells. And physical backup if things go wrong."

Lucas flipped through his cards. "I can bring the quartz nets from the shop. They're supposed to disrupt magical flow, if only for a few seconds. Could be enough to weaken her."

"I'll prep a few glyphs," Rachelle said. "The kind that dampens energy and weakens binding tethers. We'll need to draw them right before we start; chalk or ash should work."

"Salt, we need a lot of salt." Alex added.

Hudson leaned forward. "I'll handle the gear. Rope, lights, snacks, water. And maybe... a taser?"

"Pretty sure that's not how magic works," Lucas muttered, but Hudson just shrugged.

Charlotte looked at Alex. "You and I should head in first. If she senses anyone, it'll be us. She knows us the best now."

Alex gave a slow nod. "We draw her attention. Then Lucas and Hudson go for the ley point. Rachelle starts the reversal incantation. If Molga comes after her, we shield her."

"And if she tries to break the spell?" Lucas asked.

"Then we fight," Rachelle said, voice steady. "But no more than we have to."

Lucas's little brother banged on the door, yelling something about needing to charge his tablet. Lucas stood, opened the door just wide enough to slip him a five-dollar bill.

"Go away, goblin," he muttered.

Charlotte pulled out her notebook and scribbled furiously, a checklist forming in tight, neat script. "We each prep our part tonight and tomorrow. Gear, glyphs, research, intention. We meet at the side entrance of the school. 6 a.m. sharp."

"We're doing this," Rachelle whispered.

"We are all afraid, but I believe in all of you," Alex

said, glancing at each of them. "There is no one else I would rather have with me."

No one disagreed.

Saturday was coming.

And they would be ready.

Saturday morning arrived quickly. The air held a brittle, empty chill that comes just before the sun stretches high. Charlotte tightened her hoodie and glanced nervously down the alley beside the school.

The chain-link fence loomed ahead, patched in places with warped slats of wood. Beyond it: the Annex. Silent. Still. Waiting.

Lucas adjusted the bulging backpack strapped to his shoulders. "Okay, we go quickly. Over, in, down the hall, no lights."

Rachelle tugged her gloves tighter. "It might have been safer to come last night."

"More patrols at night," Hudson said, scanning the street. "At this hour, most cops are still getting donuts."

As if summoned by irony, red and blue lights flashed into existence.

"Don't. Move," came the sharp command behind them.

A patrol car glided to the curb. The officer who stepped out looked more tired than angry, but the way his hand rested on his belt said he wasn't taking chances.

"Mind telling me why five teenagers are loitering behind a school fence at six in the morning?"

None of them answered right away.

Alex cleared his throat. "We were just... uh..."

"Just what?" the officer asked, stepping closer. His partner rounded the car, eyeing the backpacks.

"Studying," Lucas offered unconvincingly. "For... a project."

"At a locked school? At dawn?"

The officer's eyebrow rose. "Let's take a look at those bags."

"Do you have a warrant, pig?" Lucas exclaimed fast without thought.

And with that statement, they were put in the back of two patrol cars.

At the Station — 7:32 A.M.

The fluorescent lights flickered overhead, casting everything in a sickly pale greenish hue. The group had been separated onto holding benches in the hallway. Still close enough to see each other, but not close enough to speak.

Lucas's bag sat opened on a metal table. A younger officer rummaged through the contents, confusion evident.

"Salt?" he asked, holding up the heavy canister like it was radioactive.

"Is this... a jar of fingernails?" said another, wrinkling his nose. "Nope. Herbs. Still weird."

"Definitely burglary tools," the first officer declared, holding up a bundle of candles, string, and iron nails." The young officer said sarcastically.

"Burglars who do aromatherapy," muttered his partner.

Charlotte sat up straighter on the bench, catching Alex's eye across the hallway. Then she brushed her nose, index finger, one tap: **"Say nothing."**

Alex gave the barest nod. Then he repeated the signal for Rachelle. She saw and passed it on to Hudson. He passed it to Lucas.

Lucas smirked and casually touched his forehead: **"Understood."**

The hum of the lights in the interrogation room was the only steady thing. Everything else buzzed with tension.

Lucas sat at the cold metal table, arms crossed, backpack slouched like a deflated animal on the floor beside the officer. His hoodie was damp from dew. His eyes, half defiant, half exhausted, watched the mirrored glass wall without blinking.

Officer Ramos leaned in from the opposite side, knuckles pressed flat on the tabletop.

"You want to explain why a thirteen-year-old is lurking behind a school before sunrise?" he asked, voice low but sharp. "Because to me, it looks like trespassing. Or worse."

Lucas stayed silent.

Another officer, Sergeant Holloway, circled behind him like a vulture, spun a chair out and sat in it sideways, arms over the backrest.

"Let's go through the contents of your little bag of secrets," Holloway said, yanking a folder open. "One set of walkie-talkies. A compass. Five candles. Three cans of salt. Hand-drawn blueprints of the school. A mirror wrapped in a red scarf. And my personal favorite, a freaking chicken bone."

Ramos lifted an eyebrow. "Planning an exorcism? Or just a really theatrical prank?"

Still, Lucas said nothing. His leg bounced under the table, but his face was stone.

"You're not stupid, Lucas," Ramos continued, tone softening in that calculated way. "You've got decent grades. No record. You don't want to throw all that away over some weird club or hazing ritual, do you?"

Lucas blinked. His jaw tightened. Still no words.

Holloway slammed the folder shut. "We can call the principal. The school board. Press charges if we feel like you're obstructing an investigation. You were on school property. You had strange materials. And you're refusing to explain why."

"We could say you were casing the place," Ramos

added. "Vandalism. Arson prep. Maybe you're part of something bigger. Want to talk about that?"

Lucas finally looked up.

Not at them.

At the mirrored glass.

He knew someone was watching.

Always was.

His voice when it came was flat but steady. "Are you done?"

Ramos blinked. "Excuse me?"

Lucas turned his head slowly, first to Ramos, then to Holloway. "I want my parents. And a lawyer."

The room fell into a thick, heavy silence.

Then Ramos leaned back, lips pressing into a hard line.

Sergeant Holloway scoffed. "Kid's got media training."

Lucas didn't move.

Didn't flinch.

He just waited.

Because if there was one thing he'd learned over the past few weeks, it was how to keep a secret, and how to protect the people it mattered to.

No matter what.

Rachelle sat stiff-backed in the metal chair, jaw tight, arms folded like armor across her chest. Her backpack, unzipped and rifled through, sat on the table like a dissection. A tangle of odd items spilled half out: chalk, matches, a rolled canvas scroll covered in symbols, and a crumpled spiral notebook filled with looping scribbles in red ink.

Officer Ramos tapped the end of a pen against the tabletop, again and again.

"You want to explain this?" he asked. His voice was calm, rehearsed, like he'd already decided how guilty she was. "Because if I were looking at this with no context, I'd say it looks like you were either planning to break in or summon something."

Rachelle didn't respond. Her gaze stayed fixed on the far wall, where a hairline crack split the concrete.

Halloway leaned forward. "6:03 a.m. That's when security cameras from the warehouse across the street, caught you at the fence. You are a smart girl, right? Honors classes. Why throw it away for something this stupid?"

Still nothing.

Ramos paced slowly behind her. "You think being quiet makes you innocent? Because I've seen plenty of smart kids get themselves expelled and arrested for less. You had open-flame materials. Salt. That notebook looks like a manifesto. Or a confession."

Rachelle smirked, barely. "You don't read much, do you?"

Halloway slapped the pen down. "Enough. We're

asking you straight: Why were you behind the school with this crap in your bag?"

She turned to look at him then. Not flinching. Not nervous. Just tired of playing along.

"You like to play tough with little girls," she said. "Is that your thing?"

Ramos moved to stand beside Halloway, crossing his arms. "You're ridiculous."

Rachelle's jaw clenched. The pressure had built slowly, like heat behind her eyes, but she didn't crack. Not here. Not like this.

She looked past them toward the mirror, the silent witness. Then she looked down at the notebook. At her own scrawled handwriting. Every line, every symbol, real. Important.

But not theirs.

"I want a parent," she said. Then, deliberately, looking Jensen square in the face: "And a lawyer."

The silence afterward was instantaneous and absolute.

Ramos exhaled, annoyed. "Of course you do."

Halloway chuckled under his breath. "They're all rehearsed. One of those damn TikTok kids."

But Rachelle just sat back in her chair, spine straight, gaze cool and steady.

She wasn't afraid of them.

They were asking the wrong questions.

And she had no intention of giving them the right ones.

Their silence only seemed to frustrate the officers more. No one confessed. No one explained the odd items — quartz, chalk, pendulum, incense, and drawn maps.

From her bench, Charlotte glanced at the clock.

8:58 a.m.

They were losing time.

Molga was waiting.

And now, the world was watching.

The police made no progress, and their superior was annoyed with the resources being tied up. It wasn't drugs or weapons, so they called their parents and cut them loose with a warning.

They thought they were in trouble before, but now their parents were coming. The lies they told were about to come undone. One by one, they were handed over to parents whose reactions bounced between annoyance and anger. They signaled each other. **"See ya Monday."**

ALEX LAY on his bed grounded, wondering what consequences his friends got. Not being able to talk was the worst; they couldn't plan or prepare. Alex felt a painful pull at his heart, another life deposit to the beast. He wasn't going to just lie here and be food. Alex turned off his light and hopped out the window.

RACHELLE'S PORCH light was off, but she opened the door before Alex could knock.

"I was thinking about sneaking to see you," she whispered, stepping aside to let him in.

"Yeah. I couldn't just sit there."

They crept to the back porch, quiet beneath the stars, with crickets chirping around them. The cool air smelled of watered lawns and distant honeysuckle.

Alex sat on the top step, rubbing his hands over his jeans. "I still blame myself."

She sat beside him. "Alex... none of us blame you."

He looked at her, eyes tired. "But it's costing us. I can feel it. Like something inside pulling tighter."

She nodded. "Me too. Like... a string tied to the middle of my chest. Every time we try to plan, every time we push forward, it pulls harder."

They sat in silence for a few breaths.

Rachelle glanced at him, wanting to ask about Charlotte. About what they found. About what had changed. But she didn't.

Instead, she reached over and took his hand. "You're not alone, Alex. We're all in this. And we're going to finish it."

His hand closed around hers. "Thanks. I needed to hear that."

They sat there under the stars, holding hands, both feeling that tightening thread, both silently promising not to let it break them.

"On Monday at school, we will need to plan." Rachelle said.

They stood and hugged each other, a solid pact that they were there for each other, and since their future was uncertain, it meant more than either would admit.

12

INTO THE FIRE

The school parking lot buzzed with idling cars and hurried goodbyes, but for the five of them, the air felt heavier, thicker, with the weight of what they weren't allowed to say.

Charlotte climbed out of her mom's car with a tight-lipped nod, her phone already surrendered for the day. Rachelle's dad didn't even slow the car to a stop before she swung the door open.

"Be smart," were his parting words. Hudson had to talk his way out of being walked to the front gate. Lucas was wearing sunglasses, probably to hide the circles under his eyes, and had stuffed his hoodie pockets with what he could salvage from their supplies his parents had taken away. Luckily they always hid his contraband in the same place.

Alex was last, backpack dragging like an anchor as he hopped down from his mom's SUV. She watched him from behind the wheel for a long second. He gave her a thumbs-up. She didn't return it and then drove off.

They converged by the side gate, the few quiet seconds they had stretching taut with things unsaid.

"No phones," Lucas said under his breath. "Grounded."

"Same," Rachelle murmured.

"Grounded," Charlotte echoed. "Forever, maybe."

Hudson shrugged. "Got a full four weeks. And a lecture about breaking and entering."

They all looked at Alex.

"I snuck out. Got caught coming back," he admitted. "Grounded and double chores."

Charlotte leaned closer, her voice soft but resolute. "We're still in this. Just... delayed."

The warning bell rang.

"We'll talk at lunch," Alex said.

As they moved through the door toward their seats in Mr. Willy's class, they looked at each other quietly, checking on each other, OK? Still in? Are you good?

Hand over heart, tap once.

Circle with forefinger and thumb.

Tap and then make a fist.

Tiny signals.

Not for plans, just for peace of mind.

Charlotte sent one toward Rachelle. Rachelle nodded back. Lucas flicked a quick I'm alive gesture to Hudson, who rolled his eyes but answered with a half-salute.

Alex looked around the room, scanning his friends as they took their seats. One by one, they met his eyes and nodded.

Even under lockdown, grounded and watched and warned... the circle held.

Lunch couldn't come fast enough.

THE CAFETERIA WAS LOUD, too loud, but the five of them had claimed a corner table behind the vending machines where sound dulled to a manageable hum. They hunched over their trays, speaking in near-whispers between mouthfuls of soggy fries and dry chicken sandwiches.

"We have to finish this," Charlotte said, her eyes flicking between each of them. "The ley point, the reversal spell, we're ready."

"I checked the lunar chart," Lucas added. "Tomorrow technically the full moon starts during the day. If we don't use the window now, it's game over. We don't have that long."

"We're unraveling," Hudson said flatly. "I felt it again last night, like my chest was empty. Like something's leaking out."

Alex nodded slowly. "We go in tomorrow. No more delays. We gather what we need tonight, and we ditch class."

"Not just any class," Rachelle said, smirking faintly. "First three. After that, it's suspicious."

Charlotte leaned forward, voice low and fierce. "We go in. We break the tether. We end Molga's hold. We take our lives back."

They all nodded, the silence between them thick with resolve.

The campus was still, half-asleep in the haze of early morning light. They'd split off from the main path, ducking between two temporary buildings before hopping the side gate with a practiced rhythm. Lucas checked his watch. 7:13 a.m. Class wouldn't start for another seventeen minutes.

They stood in front of the Annex.

Or rather, they stood in front of what used to be the door to the Annex.

Welded steel bars had been bolted over the entrance. Thick, heavy chains laced through the door handles, padlocked tight. A smear of fresh weld scars gleamed along the seams. Yellow tape fluttered nearby, stamped with DO NOT ENTER in bold black letters.

Alex stepped forward and touched the metal. It was cold. Solid. Unmovable.

"No..." he breathed.

Lucas pulled a folded multi-tool from his hoodie and poked at the welds, as if that might undo them. "This wasn't here on Monday. Someone sealed it yesterday."

"Someone knew," Rachelle said. "Someone knew we were coming."

Hudson kicked a chunk of gravel. "This is bad. Like, seriously bad."

Charlotte scanned the walls, the ground, the roofline. "There's no back entrance. No windows. No crawl space. They locked it shut and threw away the key."

Silence fell.

Alex clenched his fists. "Someone is buying time. They know we are getting close. The one that tethered her knows we found the ley point."

Charlotte reached for his hand again. "So, we find another way in."

"But how?" Hudson asked.

Lucas was already kneeling, pulling out his journal, flipping pages until he found the layout they'd drawn weeks ago.

"There is another way," he said. "The service tunnel."

Charlotte's eyes widened. "Underneath the school?"

Lucas nodded. "It's a gamble. But it might be our only shot. The passageways were found after the school was built."

They all looked at the sealed doors again, The Annex's final warning glowing in every weld, every chain.

And then they turned away. Back into the shadows. Toward a new path. Toward the dark beneath.

The wind whispered over the cracked asphalt as the five of them crept along the back wall of the old gym building, backs low, hoods up. Even though the school was starting to stir with first period bells, back here it felt like another world. Forgotten. Shadowed.

Every crunch of gravel beneath their shoes sounded like a gunshot in the silence.

"There," Hudson whispered, pointing toward the far corner.

A rusted metal hatch, half-covered by ivy and broken concrete blocks, jutted out awkwardly from the wall like an afterthought. A faint outline of where the bricks had been chipped away to make room still lingered, scarred and uneven. Just above it, nearly hidden behind a pipe, was a small engraved sign:

SERVICE ACCESS–MAINT. STAFF ONLY.

Lucas crouched beside the hatch. "I triple-checked. This leads to the substructure under the

Annex. It was used during renovations in the seventies."

Rachelle knelt beside him and peeled away the last of the ivy. A thick padlock clung to the rusted latch.

"Let me," Alex said, already fishing the small kit from his hidden flap in his backpack.

He kneeled, clicked the picks into place, and began to work. His breath slowed, lips slightly parted in concentration. The others formed a tight half-circle around him, eyes scanning the open field behind the gym. The sun was just cresting the rooftops, throwing long morning shadows across the grass.

Charlotte reached for Alex's shoulder, steadying him as a breeze picked up dust and pine needles from the eaves above.

Click.

The padlock gave way.

Alex looked up, heart pounding. "We're in."

He pulled the latch, and the hatch creaked open with a groan that set every nerve on edge. Cold air spilled out — damp, earthy, and stale, like the breath of something ancient.

One by one, they slipped inside, ducking into the darkness. Hudson pulled the hatch shut behind them, and the outside light vanished. Lucas flicked on a flashlight, its thin beam cutting across concrete walls lined with decades of spiderwebs.

The school loomed silent around them as they slipped through the passageway. Cold air rushed past them, carrying the smell of ancient stone, damp earth, and something older, something wrong.

The service tunnel swallowed the light behind them as they moved deeper, their flashlights cutting thin beams through the black. The walls were rough-hewn and cracked, heavy with moisture and lined in places with worn carvings.

Charlotte paused at a turn. "There's something ahead," she whispered.

A shimmering haze blocked the tunnel, like heat rising from asphalt, but colder. Charlotte stepped forward, breath steady, her hands rising instinctively. A translucent shield formed around her like a second skin. As she passed through the haze, the illusion dissolved with a faint sizzle. She turned and nodded. "It was a ward, trick magic. You're clear."

Next came a long passage where the ground had crumbled into a sinkhole. Jagged debris and a chasm blocked their path. Lucas stepped forward.

"I've got this."

He closed his eyes, muttering under his breath. Slowly, the void shimmered. An illusion unfolded, not just visual but tactile. A glowing bridge of light stretched across the hole. Hudson tested it with his foot. Solid.

"Just don't think about it too hard," Lucas muttered, grinning.

"Dang, Lucas, that's top-tier illusion work." Alex was seriously impressed.

They crossed quickly, the shimmer dissolving the moment Alex stepped off last.

Further in, a web of brambles, dead but thick and knotted, blocked their way. Rachelle narrowed her eyes. "Back up."

She inhaled and raised her palm. Fire sparked, then roared to life, spiraling out and licking along the dry vines. The service tunnel lit up orange as the brambles crumbled to ash.

"Smoky, but effective." Hudson coughed.

Soon, they hit another dead end: a collapsed archway and piles of stone and rubble. Hudson knelt and put his hand on the ground. "Gimme a second."

Using his enhanced strength, Hudson began hauling the largest chunks aside. Sweat beaded on his forehead. He worked quickly, grunting, until a small crawlspace was cleared through the blockage.

Alex at the rear felt it first.

A pull, not physical, not exactly, but deep and insistent, like a string hooked behind his sternum, threading through bone and blood. It tugged with a quiet urgency, not painful but impossible to ignore. His breath hitched.

"The key point," he said, barely above a whisper.

The others slowed, eyes flicking back toward him. But they felt it now too, the same invisible current stirring their nerves, drawing them inward. It was like walking into the breath of something ancient. Not malevolent, but alert. Watching.

They pressed on, boots crunching against damp stone. The tunnel widened with each step, and the air grew warmer, thicker, humid with energy that tingled against their skin. A low thrumming sound, like the deepest chord of a cello, hummed from the earth itself.

Then the corridor opened suddenly and without warning into a vast domed chamber.

The ceiling rose high above them, lost in darkness. The walls shimmered with energy, pulsing faintly. The ground sloped gently toward the center, where a natural basin of stone cradled a swirling pool of faint blue glow. It didn't glow like fire or electricity; it shimmered like memory, like thought made visible.

It wasn't like light; more like a presence.

Power radiates from the pool in rhythmic waves, pulsing steadily as a heartbeat. The surrounding air shimmered, rippling gently, like heat on asphalt. Their clothes stirred in the current. The hairs on their arms stood on end.

The ley point.

They stood in silence for a long moment, reverent,

each of them feeling something personal and unspoken. The weight of it. The invitation.

Alex stepped forward first. "Set it up."

They moved in sync now, no questions, no wasted motion, like dancers returning to familiar choreography.

Charlotte knelt and opened the pouch of salt, her fingers deft and careful. The salt poured in a white stream as she moved in a large circle around the glowing pool. Her hand didn't tremble, even as the energy pressed back. The circle was perfect.

Lucas moved to the chamber's three dark openings and raised his palms. With a flick of his fingers, illusory gates of prismatic light shimmered into being, thin veils that looked like stained glass windows stretched across shadowed archways. Color poured across the floor.

Rachelle crouched just within the circle of salt, her palms glowing soft orange. She exhaled slowly, and warmth spilled from her body in gentle waves, coaxing the clammy chill of the chamber into something bearable. Her fire didn't blaze; it breathed.

Alex walked to the very center and knelt, carefully drawing the silver chain from his pocket. The pendant, warm to the touch, almost vibrating, glowed steadily as he placed it on the stone. The moment it touched the ground, it pulsed faster, like it recognized its home.

Each of them paused.

Their breathing slowed. A hush fell. Even the chamber seemed to inhale.

Charlotte's voice was soft. "Do you feel that?"

Lucas nodded. "Like the room's... waiting."

Rachelle ran her fingers just above the floor, watching dust swirl upward. "It's listening."

Alex placed a hand over his chest. The tug was stronger now, but not uncomfortable. It felt like belonging. Like the ley line was calling something forward in him, something old, maybe even older than he was. He didn't know how to describe it, so he didn't try.

He just stood still and listened.

Then the shadows moved, not just shifting, but recoiling, like something alive was pushing through them.

The temperature dropped ten degrees in an instant. The flickering illusions cast by Lucas dimmed to embers, as if shying away from something older than light. Even Rachelle's fire crackled quieter, uncertain.

AND THEN SHE APPEARED.

Molga.

She drifted from the wall where shadow and stone met. Her arrival was not like entering a room; it was like being summoned from the bones of the earth. Darkness peeled away from her like ink lifting off water.

Her form was small, shifting at the edges, not quite solid. A silhouette of silk and midnight. Her hair floated behind her in slow coils, as if submerged in deep water. Wisps of smoke curled from her shoulders and fingers. And her eyes...

Her eyes were bottomless, black with pinpricks of white, like distant stars barely seen through a void.

She didn't step over the salt ring. She hovered just outside it, the air around her warping ever so slightly, like heat distortion. The circle held.

Her voice came as barely a whisper, but it pressed against their ears like thunder muffled behind a wall.

"You don't know what you're doing," she said softly.

"You'll doom yourselves trying."

A tremor passed through the floor beneath their feet, like the chamber itself had exhaled in fear.

Charlotte instinctively reached for Alex's arm.

Rachelle's flames danced higher for a moment, flickered, then fell still. Lucas blinked hard, trying to hold the light illusions in place, but they flickered with doubt.

Alex took a step forward, eyes locked on the dark figure.

"Then tell us what we are doing," he said. "Because we don't plan on dying."

Molga's lips curled, not quite a smile. Not quite kind.

Just knowing.

The teens flinched, but held their ground.

Charlotte stepped forward. "The gateway is feeding off us. That has to stop."

Molga's tone shifted. "I was like you once. Curious. Hopeful. Strong. But strength fades. Curiosity becomes fear. Hope turns to need. I wanted only to survive."

"You bound yourself," Rachelle said coldly. "We saw the signs. You chose this."

"I had to!" Molga snapped. "My family was gone. My name... taken. I needed help, so I wished to survive."

"And you feed off the living to keep it," Alex said.

Molga's eyes flared. "You'll never understand."

Outside the salt ring, she paced like a caged predator. "You think you've outsmarted me? That a ring of salt and some borrowed power can't stop him?"

"You can't cross the salt," Charlotte said calmly.

Molga shuddered, and the lights in the chamber flickered.

Hudson, meanwhile, cleared debris from near the ley point's edge. His hand brushed against something smooth — a jar, half-buried and wrapped in cracked leather. He lifted it slowly. Inside, suspended in darkened oil, was an old seal, and carved into the leather, almost too faint to see: "Molga Kay Everwood."

Hudson's voice trembled. "I found it. Her real name."

Molga froze.

"No..." she hissed. "That is not yours to play with!"

The energy in the chamber pulsed violently, the air thick with power. The teens braced themselves, ready.

The reversal spell was next.

And they had her name.

They were ready for whatever came next.

13

WORK THE PLAN

The chamber felt alive with pressure, magic stirring like a storm just beyond the veil of sight. The circle of salt glowed faintly under their feet. The pendant lay at the center, vibrating, its blue light casting eerie reflections across their faces.

Rachelle stood steady, chanting the first lines of the reversal spell. Her voice was calm, even as the ley energy pushed against her like wind against glass.

Hudson stepped forward, the old jar clutched in one hand, the name now burned into his memory. He looked at the trembling, furious witch beyond the salt.

Her shadow wavered. Her anger cracked.

"In the light," he said firmly, "I call you not as Molga the witch, but as your true self."

He raised his voice.

"Molga Kay Everwood."

The air snapped like a whip.

"Molga Kay Everwood."

Molga's body twitched, her feet staggering under her. The smoke of her form unraveled around the edges.

"Molga Kay Everwood!"

The name echoed like a bell across the stone chamber.

Molga gasped.

Hudson continued, "I name you and claim you."

Her eyes, once pools of black, shifted. The smoke cleared. Beneath, two human eyes blinked rapidly, hazel, flecked with gold, wide with confusion and something deeper: fear.

"I... what's happening?" she whispered, voice no longer soaked in malice. "Where am I?"

Before anyone could answer, the ley point pulsed violently.

Alex recognized Molga from his dream, the little girl tricked by a demon. In that instant, Alex realized who "he" was. "We are in trouble!"

The light turned red.

A sickening growl traveled from the entrance, the one that was bolted. The chamber floor reverberated not just with sound, but with a feeling, a vibration that rattled their bones and churned their stomachs. It was ancient and angry, older than any word they knew. Shadows jerked unnaturally toward the center of the room, sucked into a single point as the fractured stone split open with a violent crack. Light from the ley pool spasmed and flared, turning a harsh, unnatural violet.

From the hallway, footsteps echoed — slow, deliberate, and wrong. The sound bounced off stone walls and low ceilings like a countdown. A shadow spilled across the floor before they saw the figure. It stretched impossibly long, flickering with each step. Then, a silhouette. Large, human-shaped. Backlit by blinding light.

Charlotte gasped and stumbled backward. "Something's coming!"

"It's him. I tried to warn you," Molga said weakly.

A figure emerged from the glare, his face obscured by the burst of light behind him.

"You're not supposed to be here!" the voice barked.

Alex's stomach dropped. That voice. It couldn't be.

"Mr. Willy?" he called out, disbelieving.

The man stepped fully into view.

"This place is dangerous," he said, voice sharp, distorted. "You have to leave. Now."

Alex squared his shoulders, his voice shaking with fury. "We can't leave. Our lives depend on this."

In a flash, Mr. Willy lunged and grabbed Charlotte by the wrist, yanking her toward the exit. She cried out, struggling. Then, a streak of fire cracked through the air. It struck her teacher square in the chest. His shirt ignited, flames devouring cotton and silk in seconds. He didn't scream. He just snarled, face twisting into something far less human, and wiped the scorched ash from his torso with one massive hand.

Rachelle backed away, eyes wide. "He wasn't even surprised."

Molga's voice was barely a whisper. "He's here for you."

"Cover me!" Hudson shouted.

He dashed forward. Lucas's hand moved quickly. A flickering hologram of a brick wall erupted around the man holding Charlotte, momentarily disorienting him. Hudson barreled through the illusion, slamming into the figure and sending him sprawling.

He wrapped an arm around Charlotte, pulling her out of the grip. "I've got you!"

Fireballs lit up the chamber. Rachelle, arms raised, flung them one after another. Her answer for everything. Burn it! Mr. Willy's coat went up in flames, but still he rose. Charred fabric peeled away. His skin blistered, cracked, and split, yet he kept moving.

Then Alex stepped forward. He didn't shout. He didn't flinch. He focused. A cinder block flew across the room, slamming into Mr. Willy's ribs with a wet crunch. Another followed. Then another. Each struck with bone-cracking force. Finally, the dark figure staggered.

He looked up at them, eyes glowing bright, unnatural red. With one final grotesque motion, he tore the burning flesh from his own face. It peeled away like rubber.

Beneath it stood something else — a black, leathery figure, humanoid but twisted. Its skin glistened like oil. Its teeth were too sharp. Its voice, when it came again, would not be the monotone they were used to.

The room fell silent.

No one breathed.

They were no longer fighting their teacher.

They were fighting whatever had replaced him.

It spoke.

Not in any tongue they knew, but the words rumbled through the air, harsh and rhythmic, scraping like rusted chains dragged across stone. The syllables crawled into their ears, oily and cold. They couldn't understand the meaning, but the intent was carved into the air.

Mr. Willy, or whatever this was, wanted them all.

A tether — thin, ethereal, like a glowing cord — snapped taut between Molga and the ley point. She screamed, her body yanked toward the demon's waiting hand.

"No!" Hudson shouted, grabbing her. She collapsed into his arms, shaking.

The others moved fast.

"Break the tether!" Charlotte shouted.

"Buy me time!" Alex barked, already focusing.

Rachelle stepped forward, fire bursting from her hands. She hurled twin bolts at the demon's chest, the flames exploding against its hide. It roared but did not falter.

Alex clenched his fists. Stones ripped from the chamber walls and launched through the air, slamming into the demon's arm. One hit the tether, and the cord flickered, but held.

Charlotte knelt beside Hudson and Molga, forming a shimmering barrier over them. The demon clawed at it, screeching in rage, but couldn't break through.

Lucas noticed a break in the salt circle; he stepped back, hands glowing. "Hope this works…"

An illusion unfolded — mirrors and shadows — masking the salt circle entirely. To the demon's eyes, they were gone.

It stopped.

Sniffed.

Roared.

It swept its clawed hand through the space where they were… and missed.

Rachelle staggered. "How long can you hold it, Lucas?"

"Not long!"

Hudson clutched Molga tighter. She looked at him

with terrified human eyes. "I didn't know… I thought I could have my family back. I didn't know the price."

Alex turned toward the group. "The name gave her back to us. But we are not home free yet."

"We're going to get her out," Rachelle said, flame still in her palm.

The demon howled again, vile and furious.

Charlotte turned to Alex, her eyes fierce. "We need to break that tether for good."

"Then we end this," he said.

"She's slipping!" Hudson's voice cracked with desperation as he wrapped both arms tighter around Molga. Her feet were dragging across the stone floor now, the invisible tether to the demon pulling harder, like a fishing line hooked to her soul.

Molga cried out, reaching toward Hudson, toward the group. Her face contorted, not with fury or magic, but with fear. Real, human fear.

Hudson dug his heels into the floor. "I can't hold her!"

The demon reared up, enormous and full of unholy hunger, clawing at the air like a monstrous puppeteer. The tether pulsed with unnatural light. Rachelle's fire only flared harmlessly across its skin. Alex's stones pelted it like pebbles. Lucas's illusions confused it for moments, but nothing stopped its relentless pull.

They were losing her.

"He is pulling her to the ley point!" Alex yelled out.

"We're out of time!" Rachelle screamed.

Charlotte's eyes widened as she turned to Hudson. "Break the jar!"

"What?" he gasped.

"The jar!" she yelled again, voice sharp and sure. "The binding is there; break it!"

With one arm still wrapped around Molga, Hudson raised the jar overhead, slamming it down.

CRACK!

GLASS SHATTERED, magic snapped.

A shockwave exploded outward, with a sudden silence rushing in like a vacuum.

The demon jerked backward. It howled, a sickening, guttural noise that shook the walls, then staggered as if the tether it had been pulling had just been sliced in two. It clutched at the air, clawing at something no longer there. Its form flickered, losing shape.

The demon dove at them. He still had them. They felt it in their hearts as they were pulled. All of them were tethered.

"You only need one of us. Take me and let them go." Alex shouted.

"It was all my fault; it is my price to pay. I'll go willingly, free them!" Alex pleaded.

The demon considered, staring at Alex.

"Wylithar the Boundless take my deal!"

The demon laughed, a truly haunting sound, and began pulling Alex towards him.

A glimmering shield appeared around Alex. "You can't have him!" Charlotte screamed in pain.

A vortex of flame engulfed the demon. "He is ours; you cannot take him!" Rachelle shouted, tears in her eyes.

"He made the bargain; he is mine." Wylithar pulled Alex through the shield. "I cannot be denied."

Alex looked to his friends, his eyes pleading. He had made a deal to save them, but the weight of the deal was crushing.

A large piece of the cement wall hit the demon, making him stumble. "You can't have him." Hudson joined the fight.

The demon picked up Alex. "You are mine."

Charlotte looked at Rachelle, desperate; they were out of answers. Both had tears running down their faces.

The demon stepped into the gateway; he was taking Alex with him. He was waist deep in the ley when a small voice behind them said, "I release you."

It was Molga; she had dumped out the jar with their hair in it. Hudson grabbed Alex by both arms. A golden shield enveloped Alex and Hudson. The Annex became a field, bright as day. The demon stood alone. Wylithar was no longer boundless as a force from below pulled at him. The demon grabbed at the ground, trying to stay in this world.

"Now!" Alex shouted.

He lifted his arms. The entire chamber trembled. Dozens, hundreds of stone blocks from the catacomb walls ripped loose and flew across the chamber, piling over the glowing red well in the floor. A mountain of stone rose like a seal.

Charlotte came forward, drawing a glowing pattern of ancient runes in the air with her finger. They flared white and seared into the stones as if burned with a branding iron.

The gateway was sealed again.

The demon beneath the rubble gave one last roar and vanished into the ether.

Silence.

Alex dropped to one knee, exhausted. Charlotte leaned against him, trembling, her eyes still glowing faintly as the magic faded. Rachelle lowered her hands. Lucas let out a long breath. Hudson was on his knees, one arm open, reaching for Molga.

She was still there.

But no longer twisted, no longer the furious shade who'd haunted the Annex.

At the edge of the salt circle, she stood barefoot on

the stone, her hair soft chestnut, her eyes wide and innocent. She looked no older than nine.

She blinked, dazed.

"I... it's quiet now," she whispered. "I can feel the wind again. The earth. Not... him."

"Molga?" Charlotte said gently, stepping closer.

The girl nodded, smiling a very childlike smile. "I remember. When he called me, I accepted his deal. I just wanted my family back. But it wasn't them. It was never them."

Tears slipped down her cheeks. "Thank you. For setting me free."

A sudden warmth rushed through them.

Alex staggered as if something heavy had been lifted from his back. Rachelle punched Alex in the arm hard, you don't get to sacrifice yourself for me. Hudson and Lucas nodded in agreement. Charlotte echoed the sentiment; we couldn't live with ourselves if we let you pay our price. She looked at her hands. Color and strength were returning to her skin.

Their life, drained piece by piece since the first encounter, was flowing back.

They turned toward Molga.

Her childlike form began to shake, the light bending strangely around her like heat rising off pavement. She smiled once, softly and small, as if letting go of something heavy she'd carried far too long.

Then she closed her eyes.

Her hair, once chestnut brown and floating like smoke, turned silver at the roots, the color spilling downward like ink in reverse. Wrinkles bloomed across her skin like delicate cracks in porcelain. Her arms thinned, her spine curled, and her breath became shallow, tremulous.

They watched, frozen, as she aged by the second. Ten years passed in a heartbeat. Then fifty. Then hundreds. Her dress sagged around her shrinking frame. Her voice was a whisper of wind, a goodbye none of them could hear.

Charlotte covered her mouth with trembling fingers. Rachelle stepped forward, but Alex reached out to stop her gently. "Let her go," he murmured.

The girl, once a conduit of terrible power, withered into silence. Her skin faded, flaked, and folded inward. Light pulsed once from the pendant at her chest, then dimmed.

When it ended, there was nothing left but a delicate skeleton, curled gently like a child in sleep, surrounded by the glittering dust of what she had once been.

Silence filled the chamber like water.

Even the ley point pulsed softer now, like it, too, was mourning.

Hudson ran a hand through his hair, exhaling

slowly, the ever faithful protector. "That it?" he asked, voice hoarse.

Charlotte nodded slowly, her eyes glassy. "She's free now."

The silence stretched. Then Lucas stepped forward, his voice just above a whisper. "We did it."

No cheers. No high-fives. Just a shared, aching awe.

Rachelle knelt beside the bones, setting a small flame to burn gently near them, a quiet, flickering tribute.

Alex looked at each of them in turn. Their clothes were torn. Their faces were marked with soot, sweat, and magic. But their eyes were clear. Changed.

They stood in a wide circle, shoulder to shoulder. Tired. Humbled. Alive!

And for the first time in a long while, free.

Alex stepped forward slowly, his gaze lingering on the fragile remains.

"We should find her family," he said quietly. She deserves to go home." He gathered her bones carefully into his backpack and hid them in a dark alcove. Once we find out where her family is buried, we will be back.

As Alex stood up, he shoved something into his pocket.

14

FACE THE MUSIC

The rusted catacomb door creaked open, and sunlight struck their faces for the first time in hours. Alex squinted, shielding his eyes with one hand. The others filed out behind him, scraped, dusty, and exhausted, but alive.

And changed.

Then he saw them.

Two men in gray polo shirts stood on the far side of the annex wall, arms crossed, radios clipped to their belts. Their old golf carts sped towards them. |

Campus Security.

"Oh no," Charlotte whispered.

Lucas groaned, "Really? Now?"

The guards jumped out of their cart and marched

toward them. "Don't move. We have been looking for you."

As if they needed that pointed out. They were busted again. They got on the carts and were driven to the office.

Soon, they were led through the admin hall like a group of fugitives. Students whispered and stared.

In the principal's office, Mr. Prescott gave them a look that was neither angry nor smug, just tired.

"We called your parents when you weren't in class," he began, folding his hands on the desk. "Each one assured us you were on campus, so we checked around. That's when we found the annex door."

His eyes narrowed. "Tampered with."

No one spoke.

"You're lucky you didn't hurt yourselves. But this isn't just a prank. This is dangerous. You're getting five days of in-school suspension. You'll report here first thing tomorrow morning."

They were each released to their parents — some of whom were furious, others silent, all disappointed — again.

Alex barely said a word on the drive home. The minute he stepped inside, his mom pointed upstairs.

He spent the rest of the day in his room, grounded indefinitely.

Lying flat on his back, Alex stared at the uneven pattern of glow-in-the-dark stars stuck to his ceiling. Most were peeling at the edges. One hung on by a single corner, a tiny comet barely holding on.

The room was still, too still. The kind of quiet that pressed down on his chest.

His phone was gone. His door was shut. The usual hum of music or video game chatter was absent. Just him, a box of guilt he couldn't open, and a heart that still felt the pull of something far older than he could name.

They had done it.

They'd broken the curse.

They'd freed Molga.

And they'd gotten caught.

Five days of suspension. Parental lockdown. One shot to the face of normal.

He folded his hands over his stomach and exhaled slowly.

The smell of salt still clung to his hoodie. He hadn't washed it and hadn't wanted to. It felt like the only thing left tying him to what had happened. The fight, the power, the darkness. Molga's real name echoed through the service tunnel like a song that had always been waiting.

"Molga Kay Everwood..."

She had cried when she was freed. Not with words, but with her face. The little girl they'd found at the end of it all wasn't a monster.

She was just a memory... unraveling.

And now... she was gone.

All that magic. All that risk. The lies, the fear, the stolen moments under the school and in between the seconds of ordinary life.

And now he was grounded.

Probably for life.

He didn't even blame his parents. They weren't wrong.

He had lied.

A lot.

And what would he have said anyway?

"Sorry, Mom, I had to confront a soulbound witch, and a demon tied to an underground ley point beneath the school. But we fixed it. Oh, and I have telekinesis now. Pass the cereal?"

No, they wouldn't believe him. Nobody would. But the others would. Charlotte. Rachelle. Lucas. Hudson.

He smiled a little.

Rachelle.

She had held his hand that night on her porch like she meant it. Like she got it. All of it. She didn't blame him. Even after everything.

And Charlotte...

His heart stuttered at the memory of her lips on his, soft and unexpected at the threshold of the Annex. That moment had been his, and hers, and he wasn't sure what it meant yet.

But it meant something.

He rolled onto his side, then reached into the drawer beside his bed. He hadn't planned to look again. Not tonight. But the warmth had returned earlier, like a whisper in his pocket.

He opened his palm.

Molga's necklace.

Pale and smooth, sitting on his skin like a monument to their struggle.

It wasn't just a necklace.

It was proof.

That it had been real. That they had survived it. That he had done something that mattered.

The necklace was his reminder.

Of power.

Of friendship.

Of everything they couldn't say out loud.

Alex closed his hand around it and exhaled into the darkness.

He had thought that ending the curse would bring a wave of relief. Maybe a celebration.

Instead, he felt drained.

The room was quiet. The kind of quiet that makes your thoughts louder.

He rolled onto his side, wondering what Charlotte was doing right now. What Rachelle had told her mom. Whether Hudson was already halfway through a lecture from his dad. If Lucas had managed to joke his way into a bigger punishment.

It hadn't been a dream. Not a shared hallucination or collective hysteria.

Later, Alex sat cross-legged on the carpet of his bedroom, an old leather jacket draped across his lap. It was too small now, cracked at the seams, stiff from years buried in the back of his closet. He hadn't worn it in forever. Now it would serve a different purpose.

A small utility knife rested beside him, along with a single glass jar, clear and ordinary; its cork texture appeared old and weathered. It looked harmless, like something his mom might've used for perfume. But Alex knew what it would become.

With slow, careful hands, he cut rectangular pieces from the back of the jacket. The leather gave reluctantly, releasing its warm, dusty scent into the room. He trimmed the leather into a pouch to fit the jar, binding it tight around the neck of the jar. The leather creaked as he cinched it, rough under his fingers, familiar in a way that ached.

He wound black thread stitching holding the leather tight around the lid, knotting it with deliberate care. Not fancy. Not perfect. But steady. His own pattern. His own spell.

It wasn't finished yet, not until he had the hair. One lock from each of them: Lucas, Hudson, Charlotte, Rachelle. And his own. Five locks to seal inside, woven together. That would make it real. That would make it theirs.

For now, the jar sat empty, waiting. Alex brushed his thumb over the glass, imagining their faces. Lucas, steady but quiet. Hudson, laughing too loud. Charlotte, thoughtful, frowning when she didn't mean to. Rachelle, seeing straight through him with those eyes that seemed older than hers should be. He smiled faintly, though the weight of everything pressed down hard on his chest.

He reached for Molga's necklace, where it lay coiled on the nightstand. The metal was cold against his skin as he slipped it over his head. The instant it touched his chest; a shiver ran through him. The room tilted, heavy and light at once, and then, magic.

Not a spark, not a flare. Just a pulse, deep and low, like a second heartbeat syncing with his own. His vision shimmered at the edges, the jar lifting gently from the carpet as though carried by a hidden current. Alex didn't gasp or flinch; he only watched with his breath held as it floated slowly across the room. The jar came to rest on his desk with a faint tap, as though it had always belonged there.

Alex let out the breath, realizing how tired he was. His hand lingered against the necklace, fingers brushing the cold curve of metal.

Not cursed.

Not normal.

Changed.

And no matter what came next, they would face it together.

Tomorrow, he'd find the right time. A quiet moment, away from the eyes of teachers and detention monitors. He'd pass it to them, no big ceremony, no long explanation.

Just a gesture.

A way of saying I see you.

We're still us.

This mattered.

Alex leaned back against the bed and looked at the ceiling.

And for the first time in days, he let himself smile. It was all real. The annex. The magic. The curse. Molga.

The necklace sat under his palm like a charm from another world, a world they had stepped into, fought through, and barely escaped from.

Alex closed his hand gently around it, and for the first time that day... he smiled.

HE LAY IN BED, his burdens having begun to slip from his shoulders. As he nodded off, Alex slipped into a dream.

At first, it was only light. Not blinding, but soft, like the warmth of the late afternoon sun spilling through curtains. It filled everything, gentle and golden, humming in his bones. Then the scene took shape, as dreams do: a field, endless and open, wildflowers swaying in a quiet breeze that smelled like honey.

There, in the center of it all, stood Molga.

Not the version twisted by shadow and centuries of pain. Not the girl who hovered between child and curse.

She was whole now.

Young again, at their age, with soft curls the color of chestnut tumbling down her back. Her eyes were no longer bottomless wells of sorrow, but warm and bright like a summer evening sky. She wore a simple white dress, loose and flowing, and her bare feet brushed the grass.

And she was not alone.

A man and woman stood beside her, hands clasped in hers. Her parents. Alex could see it in the way the woman smiled down at her with tears in her eyes, and the way the man stood just slightly in front of them, protective even in peace. Both dressed in clothes long faded by time, yet glowing with ethereal light.

A little boy raced around them, laughing, a younger brother maybe, or a memory of one lost long ago. He wore a hat made of woven reeds and kept trying to put it on Molga's head, giggling when it slipped over her eyes.

Molga laughed.

A sound Alex had never heard from her before — not wicked, not bitter, just pure joy, clear and bell-like. She tossed her head back, light catching her face, and smiled toward the sky.

Then her eyes turned right to him. She saw him. She knew him. No fear. No anger. Just gratitude. Quiet and true. Thank you, her lips said, though no sound came.

And Alex nodded.

His chest ached, not with sorrow, but with something brighter. Closure. Forgiveness. Peace. The heavy knot in his heart unraveled, replaced by the calm certainty that she was where she belonged. Whole. Loved. Free.

A breeze passed through the field, scattering petals and glimmers of light. The dream began to fade, the golden horizon stretching out like an invitation.

Just before everything turned to white, Molga raised her hand in farewell.

Not a goodbye.

But a blessing.

Alex woke with tears on his cheeks and a steady beat in his chest. He would never forget her. And somehow, he knew, she would never forget them either.

15

REST IN PEACE

The school was quieter than usual, a gray hush hanging over the buildings like fog. The five of them met just past the rusted front gate, with no plan, no messages. Just instinct. Like magnets, they pulled together.

Charlotte arrived first, backpack slung over one shoulder, the faint bruise on her temple barely visible beneath her hair. She leaned against the concrete post, biting her thumbnail and watching the parking lot. Then came Rachelle, hoodie pulled up, fingers twitching slightly like they still remembered fire.

Hudson trailed in next, jaw set, earbuds in, nodding without a word.

Lucas walked with his hands jammed in his coat

pockets, eyes darting toward the sky every few seconds like he expected it to change.

And then Alex, last, but only by seconds. His face was pale, but his eyes were brighter than usual, like sleep had never come but dreams had.

They didn't speak at first. They didn't need to. Then Lucas exhaled, breaking the silence. "Detention. What a hero's welcome!"

Charlotte snorted. "Could've been suspension."

"Could've been expulsion," Hudson added, stretching his arms behind his head. "We kinda breached a hole to the underworld."

"Could've been death," Rachelle said flatly. She wasn't joking.

Alex nodded once, then looked at them all. "I had a dream last night."

That got their attention.

He cleared his throat and stepped closer, his voice low, like the words were precious. "Molga was... there. In this field. There was sunlight, and wind, and flowers, so many flowers. She was with her family. Her real one. Laughing. Smiling.

She looked whole. Human. Like she was finally... herself.

Rachelle's breath hitched. "I saw her too."

Charlotte turned. "You did?"

Rachelle nodded slowly. "Mine was different. She

was near a river. Sitting on a dock with her feet in the water, humming. She wasn't alone. There were people, souls maybe? They all looked... healed. And she looked at me. Like she knew we helped."

Lucas's lips pressed together. "Mine was like... a garden. This huge, endless place. She was planting things, just calmly, like it was the most natural thing in the world. She was older in mine. Not old, just... grown. Like the girl she could've been if she'd lived normally. Peaceful."

Hudson blinked at them all. "Okay, this is weird, because I had one too. She was dancing. In the woods. Just moving around like wind, and there were lights everywhere. I remember laughing. Like I felt what she felt."

They all turned to Charlotte.

She hesitated. Then, softly: "Mine was quiet. Just her and a candle in the dark. But the dark wasn't bad. It was... rest. Like she was watching over something precious."

Alex looked down, his voice cracking slightly. "We didn't just save her."

Charlotte stepped closer. "She saved us too."

Lucas rubbed his eyes. "I mean, not to ruin the mood, but... that was real, right? All of that? The dreams? The chamber? The demon?"

"It was real," Hudson said. "Too real."

Rachelle kicked at the sidewalk. "And we all made it out."

"We did more than survive," Alex said. "We held it together. Even when it got insane. We were more than just scared kids with weird powers."

Charlotte nodded. "We trusted each other."

Lucas shrugged. "We saved each other."

"And her," Rachelle whispered. "We gave her something she hadn't had in three hundred years."

They stood in a loose circle, shoulders slouched from exhaustion, eyes rimmed with shadows, but something stronger wove through them now. Not just trauma. Not just memory. Bond. Bonded by trial. Bonded by the dark and the flame and the blood and the fear. Bonded by choice.

Alex glanced at the time. "We should probably go face our punishment."

"Detention never looked so noble," Lucas muttered.

Hudson offered a mock bow. "After you, my liege."

Charlotte laughed under her breath. "Let's just not get expelled before graduation."

They started walking. Five kids who weren't just kids anymore. Five friends who had stepped into the dark... and come back different. Changed. Marked. Connected. And maybe, just maybe, ready for whatever came next.

The overhead lights buzzed with fluorescent apathy,

casting a dull gray tone across the detention room. Mismatched desks formed a half-hearted circle in the middle, their metal legs scraping the floor like reminders of forgotten battles. In the corner, behind a cluttered desk, the detention monitor scrolled lazily through his phone, earbuds in, barely pretending to supervise.

Five students sat in the circle, slumped, silent, each carrying the weight of more than just bad decisions.

Charlotte had her hoodie pulled up and head leaned back, arms crossed, eyes shut tight as if sleeping could erase the past week. Hudson sat beside her, mirroring her posture, chin dropped, mouth slightly open, already drifting.

Lucas balanced a paperback on his knee, face neutral, but his eyes moved too fast for anyone truly reading. Rachelle doodled absently on her folder, flame-colored hair falling across her face, hiding her expression. Alex sat perfectly still, eyes flicking from one to the other.

He moved his fingers subtly.

"Five days."

Lucas noticed first, nodding slightly. He flashed back.

"Grounded for a month."

Charlotte opened one eye.

"Phone's gone."

Rachelle gave a tiny shrug.

"Life sentence."

They shared faint, humorless smiles. It was all ridiculous, but also very real. Five days of in-school suspension. Five days of silent lunches, missed classes, and zero privacy.

Alex turned toward Rachelle. Her foot tapped the floor, restless, the only sign of the fire inside her.

He signaled again. **"Quiet. Don't attract attention."**

She nodded once, but her brow furrowed with curiosity. Her gaze sharpened.

Alex exhaled slowly and opened his palm. A small black jar rose weightlessly from his skin. It crossed the room quietly.

Rachelle's eyes widened as the object hovered toward her. She reached up slowly, reverently, and closed her fingers around it. She looked at Alex. He made a scissor motion with his fingers to his hair and floated a pair of scissors to her.

She closed her eyes and cut a piece of hair and put it in the jar.

A warm glow pulsed faintly from her hand. Then, with a smirk, she held up one finger. Flame danced on the tip like a candle waiting for breath.

Lucas blinked in surprise, snapping the book shut with a soft thwap. He glanced toward Alex, eyebrows raised.

Alex's fingers moved again. **"Stay quiet."**

Alex floated the jar from Rachelle's desk to land softly in Lucas's waiting palm. Lucas gave a slow grin as the scissors followed. He quickly cut a piece of hair and put it in the jar. He felt the familiar warmth and reached out into the room around them.

A ripple shimmered in the air like the shimmer of a bubble. Suddenly, the five teens were hidden from the eyes of the monitor, their presence blurred in the corner of his eye. To him, they were just quiet kids slumped in detention.

Lucas turned and gave Charlotte a light tap on the shoulder. She stirred, blinking, then sat up. Hudson followed, rubbing his face with a groggy hand.

Lucas handed the jar and scissors to Charlotte. Hudson and Charlotte both couldn't believe Alex had his powers.

Charlotte shivered as her hair fell into the jar. "I feel it," she mouthed. She handed the jar and scissors to Hudson, as she felt the warmth build inside her.

Hudson cut his hair, putting it in the jar. "I feel it again," he signed, his face lighting up with a new kind of energy. He held up the jar, letting Alex levitate it back to him. Alex corked the bottle, putting it back in his backpack.

They all looked at Alex.

Their powers had returned.

Even inside this dull room with its sticky floor, buzzing lights, and the faint smell of someone's leftover lunch... something had shifted.

They weren't just grounded teens serving time anymore.

They were a circle of power, reborn in silence.

EPILOGUE

lex stared at the group chat.

The typing dots popped up fast.

they took my weights. Alex do you understand i'm weightless!

Charlotte:

Tell him he's being dramatic.

Lucas:

Alex. Seriously. Wait.

Whatever it is can happen tomorrow.

Alex didn't respond right away. He reread their messages, feeling the familiar knot tighten in his chest. Then he typed, slower this time.

Alex: I think I found where Molga's family is buried.

Alex: She's been alone a long time.

Alex: She needs to go home.

There was a pause in the chat. A long one.

Hudson: ...dang.

Lucas: :(

Charlotte: You shouldn't go alone.

Alex: I have to.

Alex: I think she's waiting.

After a short moment.

Rachelle: I'm coming with you.

An hour later, the halls of the school were silent again. Just like that first morning, when this all began.

Rachelle met Alex outside her house, and they walked to school. She didn't ask why he needed to do this, or what they'd tell the others later. She just handed him a flashlight and whispered, "Let's go."

They were quiet mainly because they were tired of getting caught. They ducked under the ivy and reached the catacomb door. The large welds covered every seam.

"Well crap," Rachelle let out with a sigh.

"It's okay." Alex put his arm around her, levitated them up and through a broken window, and lowered them softly to the ground inside the Annex.

"You've gotten good," she said as she made a flame big enough to light the whole area.

They moved carefully through the shadows, past crumbling bulletin boards and quiet lockers, until they reached the sealed wing. Alex knelt beside the alcove they had hidden Molga's bones in. She was wrapped gently in cloth inside his backpack.

HE HELD them as if they were something sacred.

"I think I remember where the old cemetery used to be," he said. "She told me... She showed me."

THEY WALKED QUIETLY, two shadows under the stars, following old paths no one remembered.

At the edge of town, past the last broken fence and forgotten trail, the land opened into a clearing. No markers. No stones. Nothing but wind and weeds.

"This is it," Alex whispered.

Rachelle took the amulet from around her neck, held it out, and closed her eyes.

The amulet pulsed faintly. Then began to glow, soft and steady.

She walked forward, step by step, until the glow brightened, then stopped. "Here," she said. They dug together, hands in dirt, hearts in the past. When they finished, Alex laid the bones gently in the earth. "You're home now," he whispered.

The wind stirred.

Then, light.

A soft shimmer formed beside them, rising like mist, until it took shape. A small figure in an old-fashioned dress. Hair tied back in ribbons. Bare feet, dusty with time.

Molga.

She looked at them both with eyes full of peace.

And smiled.

She stepped forward, hugged Rachelle first, light, warm, and real.

Then turned to Alex. "Thank you," she said, her voice like wind chimes and spring.

He hugged her back, even as she began to fade.

"I'll remember you," he whispered.

"I know," she said.

And then she was gone.

Alex and Rachelle stood in silence for a long time.

Eventually, he looked at her, eyes shining but calm. "You didn't have to come."

"Of course I did," she said. "You're my person."

He took her hand.

They walked home like that — quiet, tired, and a little changed.

Not just because of ghosts or annexes or secrets buried in time.

But because tonight something had finally made right.

AUTHOR'S NOTE

Thank you so much for taking the time to read Alex in the Annex. This story was actually born during one of those long car rides with my son, Miles. He's planning to be an author too, and honestly, he already has a stronger handle on writing conventions than I do. We love to brainstorm together, tossing around ideas until something sticks. I can still remember when we first talked through the premise for Alex.

At its heart, the story came from this feeling of wanting to escape. My whole life, I've imagined having a superpower, anything from flying to reading minds. I think that longing was connected to always knowing I was "different," even if I didn't know why. I could read faces, solve puzzles quickly, visualize things so vividly that I could "practice" in my head and then perform them almost perfectly the first time in real life.

And yet, despite those abilities, I struggled in school. Honestly, I thought I was dumb. It wasn't until college that I realized, wait a minute, other people were struggling with things that came easily to me. Slowly, it dawned on me that I wasn't dumb after all. I was just wired differently.

Then, just last year, I was officially diagnosed with severe ADHD and dysgraphia. That diagnosis was a revelation; it explained so much. The spelling mistakes, the awful handwriting, the difficulty turning thoughts into words on a page. For fifty-five years I had been coping through trial and error, masking, and hiding the parts of myself I thought set me apart.

Now, with medication, coaching, and self-understanding, the stories in my head have finally found a way out. Seeing characters who once lived only in my imagination come alive on the page, it feels like magic. I get goosebumps sometimes. It's transformative, like I can finally set down some of the masks I've been carrying.

The most rewarding part is hearing from readers who say they feel that same spark I felt while writing. To know that my words can transfer emotion, that someone else can catch the energy I poured into a story — that's pure joy.

So thank you for joining me on this journey. I have so many more stories to share, and time permitting, I'll get them to you as quickly as I can. Next up: Aries I– The King of Mars.

ACKNOWLEDGMENTS

Lizzie Pahl – For taking time out of your already busy schedule of two job and your own writing, to read my story, point out its weaknesses, giving detailed advice to help make it better.

Jo Armitage – The best editor, thank you for your time and talent. You continue to make me a better writer. I appreciate the way you patiently put up with my inexperience.

Chloe Maey – Many thanks for talking through ideas with my you allowed me to explore possibilities in the storyline.

Miles Scholz – For letting me brainstorm with him and letting me share in his ideas.

Vanessa Valenbaer - For being supportive with me and taking the time to answer all my many questions about how to present a respectful witch character.